GALAXY'S END

DAVID ANDRUS

KIMBERLY ANDRUS

Tellwell Talent
www.tellwell.ca

ISBN
978-0-2288-6053-2 (Paperback)
978-0-2288-6054-9 (eBook)

For my loving father, my mentor, my idol, I love and miss you every moment of every day. The world keeps moving forward...

Kimberly Andrus

CHAPTER ONE

In his first book, *The Grand Return,* Professor Carter James went into great depth about "The Creation of the Word", writing an entire chapter under that title. But I doubt that he was talking about my machine, the Linotype machine.

Professor James had something else in mind when he stated in epigrammatic fashion that "the word is created for its own purpose, in spite of the writer's intended use it."

In the media the professor has been compared to Marshall McLuhan, but is said to be McLuhan's antagonist, or disputant, depending on which commentator you read. The dust jacket of *The Grand Return* claims that McLuhan buried the printed word, and Carter James came to praise it.

The book was heavy going for a mere printer like me, even one considered to belong to the intelligentsia of the trade, primarily because a typesetter was expected to know how to spell, how to use a dictionary, and how to break a word.

My interest in *The Grand Return* came four years after Galaxy Press closed its doors and returned me to a workplace crowded with people thrown out of this job by technology. And this was Professor James' single-minded and unrelenting cause – to promote a return to a time when men had closer relationships to machines than they did to women. He characterized this period as the height of the Great Machine Age. Professor James was fond of capitalizing his pronouncements to make sure his readers got the point.

It is such comments that still makes the skinny, nervous classics teacher a popular guest on talk shows, and the subject of magazine articles. He is one of the first prophets of the new millennium and his cry for a return to the past is a pleasant contrast to the frightening newness of the present, which is so unstable it transforms into the future before you can spell or speak the word. The professor, with great contempt, expresses it nicely in the word "presenture".

The newness is subsiding quickly, of course, but the first few years have been alive with the taut sensibilities of the end-of-the-century angst that is not very far behind us.

Yet when I first tried to read the professor's rant, which wanted to carry me back to the decisive year of 1976, my thoughts lingered on more recent times. Galaxy Press, the printing shop where I worked, had effectively extended 1976 to 1999. Its last year, and the Final Year of the Last Millennium. (It's difficult not to follow Professor James' Urge to Capitalize after reading him for a while.)

The professor compared 1976 to the American Revolution of 1776, claiming that nothing was the same after the two dates. For my trade this was certainly true. Even by 1976 computer technology had almost replaced printing from raised type – then called letterpress printing, now referred to as "old era printing".

Galaxy Press was spared by its owner, Simon Goldberg, from what he saw as an enormous flood of change, a flood that he consciously linked to the Holocaust he had survived in Poland. He believed that both events occurred as part of a historical process designed to submerge, drown, and dissolve the past.

Oddly, Professor James makes very few references to the swift transmutation of printing from lead to electricity. This omission can only be accounted for by the simple fact that Carter James never held a solid line of lead type in his hand. He never skimmed the hot, silvery surface of molten lead on a Linotype machine, with the awareness that all meaning existed in this mutable, primary fluid.

I did both every working day, until Galaxy Press, like the century itself, closed its doors for good.

"It's just a bloody machine," Felix Mason said. "Like any other machine."

Mason stood beside me, making it difficult to turn in my chair to look up at him. I brought my hands back to the keyboard, and my eyes to the paper on the copy holder. I touched a few keys, and the brass letters clattered into the assembler.

But Mason did not leave. He lit a cigarette and blew smoke at my machine.

I shifted the chair back from the keyboard and looked up at him. Felix Mason was not a big man, but he carried himself as if he were. Standing, he seemed casually aggressive, a half-smirk on his lips, arms crossed.

"What I don't get, is why you call it '*the machine*'," he said. "As if no other machine qualifies to be called a machine."

I stood up, stepped away from Mason, refusing to be intimidated. The machine stood higher than both of us.

"You must know," I said, half-serious, "that the Linotype is the intellectual heart of the trade."

Mason laughed shortly.

"You even keep a straight face," he said.

"What do you want?"

He held out his hand, and I took the two short lines from him.

"The gripper caught them," he said.

I looked at the face of the type. A clean, sharp indentation ran across the printing face of both lines. I sighed heavily.

"I have to change the magazine," I said. "Do you need it right now?"

"It's on the press," he said flatly. "Or should I say, it's on 'my machine'?"

"Funny. Move out of the way."

I had no choice. When a pressman destroyed the type, it had to be replaced right away – he could do nothing until he had the new lines.

I lifted the heavy magazine off the machine and carried it to the steel rack behind me. I pulled out another magazine and loaded it onto the machine. After I had typeset the new lines, I would have to change the magazine back again.

"Try not to destroy these," I said to Mason, as I handed him the new lines, still hot from the mold.

Mason dropped his cigarette butt on the old hardwood floor, and stepped on it, then walked away.

Within an hour, Mr. Goldberg was at my machine, holding several lines of my type in his hands. "Can you fix it?" he asked.

Mr. Goldberg stood so close to me I could smell what he had for lunch – sweet, canned peaches, and an egg salad sandwich. The blandness of the mayonnaise lingered in the air around him. He was leaning over to see what the problem was, but Mr. Goldberg was even less mechanically inclined than I was. I had opened the vise frame of the machine so that we both could see the parallel trimming knives. I stared at the side of his face. The owner of Galaxy Press was in his late seventies, and the veins in his temple stood out, ugly and dangerous looking.

"Can you get the mechanic in?" I asked.

Mr. Goldberg straightened and adjusted his belt over his soft belly. He shook his head slowly.

"Floyd's sick," he said. "The diabetes is getting into his eyes."

This was bad news. Floyd was the only good Linotype mechanic in the area, which included the entire city of Toronto. The only other mechanic, who had also owned a large inventory of parts, had quit the business, and sold everything to an American firm two years before. My machine was suddenly a mechanical flower without a stalk, and soil to support it.

"So can you fix it?" Mr. Goldberg asked again.

I leaned back in my chair, "I can try," I said. "I've already tried once – but I'll get to work on it."

It bothered me to see the forlorn look on Mr. Goldberg's face. He was worried about the lack of help for the machine. I knew he loved the old model No. 8. He had picked it out himself when a small-town newspaper had gone under in the sixties.

He rested his hand on top of the machine's first elevator, and I instinctively put my left hand on the clutch handle to make certain it was disengaged. In spite of the old man's love for the machine, I always became nervous when he, or anyone else stood too close to the casting area.

"Harvey says he can't lock up the lines when they're off their feet," he said after a moment.

"And Felix can't print them when they're smashed," I said. I was hurt by Mr. Goldberg's observation, which was also meant as criticism. A good Linotype operator wouldn't allow his lines of type to get off their feet, to become more narrow at the bottom than at the top.

"I'll get on it right away," I said, hoping this time he would move away and let me get on with my job. This was something between the machine and me, something I wanted to solve myself. Finally, Mr. Goldberg nodded. The veins in his temples subsided a little.

"Let me know how you make out," he said. "If you have a problem. Elizabeth worries about the down-time."

Elizabeth. I glanced towards the office, and through the smeared and cracked glass I saw the secretary bent stiffly over her desk. Was *he* afraid of her too?

Mr. Goldberg patted the top of the elevator mechanism once more, nodded again, and moved away, tugging at the waist of his pants.

I looked over at Harvey Wells, who stood beside his make-up stone with his hands on his hips, watching me. Sonofabitch. I knew he had gone to the boss, and I hated him intensely for this. We had already discussed the problem with my type, so why did he have to go to the boss? But of course, he too had probably recorded some down-time at his end and had to answer to Elizabeth Begg.

We were almost successful in acting as if our work still mattered. As if our existence in Galaxy Press was something more than an elaborate performance, complete with costumes and machinery from a black and white period film. No one, however, had come into Galaxy Press to make a movie. The very real grime of the shop would have turned them away. The dust and chemicals in the air, a natural part of our lives, would have choked them.

It seems curious now that everything of importance took place in the last year of Galaxy Press' existence. It was also the last year of the century, and the last year of the millennium.

Everything, of course, that happened that year can be seen as significant simply because a thousand-year period was ending. Throughout the last century there was an almost fanatical fascination with first things. Great attention was given to the first man to climb Mount Everest, the first man on the moon, the first test tube baby, the first black politician, the first woman member of parliament, the first woman prime minister, and the first gender-confused leaders of business and politics.

Then the craze turned to last things. The last baby of the Second Millennium has become a ludicrous controversy – whether it was Willy Jones of Gooseneck, Sarah Stern of Israel, or Juan Sanchez of the Philippines. Or one of the six thousand pretenders to the position.

None of the last things seems as important to me as my own position in history, just as I'm sure everyone alive has their own personal, and particular claim to uniqueness on the eschatological clock. I haven't yet been challenged about my claim to be the last Linotype Operator of the Twentieth Century. Just as I had once claimed – in my own mind, at least – that I was the best operator alive, anywhere. I saw no reason not to claim to be the last operator. Why not? Nobody cared anyway. Nobody listened.

Except Kitty.

"You and the Neanderthals," she said. "They could prop you up next to the exhibit in the Science Centre."

Kitty said this shortly after we had become lovers, in that time when lovers say many things, things that later would be seen as silly, cruel, or even vicious.

Galaxy Press without doubt was one of the last functioning letterpress print shops in the western world, one of the last to use lead in almost everything it did. Lead was the *prima materia* printers had worked with since Gutenberg's invention of movable type in the fifteenth century. And ironically – or so it seemed to me – it was a man with *berg* in his name who owned the last shop, and very nearly closed the millennium with it. Johannes Gutenberg started my trade in 1440, and Simon Goldberg ended it 500 years later. Mr. Goldberg's reasons for maintaining the shop and keeping alive its old era craftmanship were tragic, and it is understandable why he nourished this illusion of timelessness. What is less understandable is why the rest of us, mostly journeymen printers, went along with it. We all knew that Galaxy Press would soon come to its inevitable end, and we would have to find jobs in a world that had become digitalized, and feminized, a world that required skills that most of us did not possess. I, perhaps, less than anyone else.

"Why on earth do you stay there?" Kitty repeatedly asked.

My answers were never good enough for her, probably because there really were no adequate answers.

"It's what I know how to do," I usually said. "What I have to do." This invariably brought a contemptuous laugh from Kitty.

Once I got to know her, I was struck by the visible signs of age that were appearing on Kitty's face, and on her body. When she and Felix Mason were lovers, I saw her only at a distance, both emotionally and physically. Those times, when she appeared in the shop, she was a striking figure. In her early forties, she still had the slenderness of her youth, and she wore colourful blouses and skirts that attracted attention and undisguised lust wherever she went. She later would laugh at this and say, "Why shouldn't I dress show I feel like dressing? It's not my problem if men react like dogs in heat."

Kitty also knew how to stand, and from across the shop, and from behind my machine, I could watch her as she talked and flirted with Mason. I watched how she stood, and how she held her head, and lightly tossed her shoulder-length hair. Kitty had high cheekbones, and wide-set grey eyes. She was both beautiful and, in a curious way, handsome, and more than once, watching her from behind my machine, I felt the familiar stirring that seemed to happen by itself, as if in darkness the blind could see. Later, up close, I saw more of the truth. The freckles on her breasts, and their softness. There was softness too, in the flesh of her throat, an area I liked to linger over, and kiss gently. I liked it because Kitty claimed that after her first orgasm such kissing gave her two or three smaller orgasms, "like a roller-coaster going over bumps," she said. At the corners of her eyes there was a permanent redness, as though the delicate flesh was irritated.

"Twentieth-century disease," she said when I pointed it out to her.

"Then it won't last long," I said. For some reason, any mention of the cosmic movement of the times aroused something in Kitty.

"Do you want me to do it now?"

This always ended further conversation, and further close study of one another's physical being. At least for me. This was when Kitty acted in contradiction to everything else, she presented herself to be.

"What *exactly* does 'miscellaneous' *mean*?"

Like Mr. Goldberg, Elizabeth Begg usually stood so close I couldn't operate the machine properly. If the machine jammed and slashed, she could get a squirt of molten lead directly in the face, or on her flat chest.

Elizabeth Begg was skinny, and suffused with nervous and chemical energy, so that after a few seconds a slight tremble began to move through her body. When I turn my head, I found her greenish eyes locked onto me, her lined face set into a grim, tight expressionless mask. The skin of her through, though strained was soft with age, and a double strip of loose skin ran from beneath her chin to where her collarbones came together.

"Miscellaneous can mean all sorts of other things," I said, in case she had forgotten what I had just told her.

"Such as?"

"Checking the spelling of words, or where a syllable divides, or correcting a widow."

She snorted at the last term. Elizabeth Begg didn't think it was important to avoid having a tiny, single word appear alone at the top of a new page. I'm certain that in some obscure way she believed I used the term to berate, and possibly humiliate her personally, that it reflected somehow on her own widowhood of 20 years.

I found that if I kept calm, and fiddled with the machine, clicking the vice-block handles, or changing all the settings – or best, rearranging the letters on the sorts rack – she would relent and stalk off with a comment thrown over her shoulder, something sharp, usually about how I should use a dictionary to look up miscellaneous.

Mr. Goldberg fully supported his secretary, though when things got too hot, he usually acted as arbitrator, and placated everyone by seeming to take Elizabeth Begg's side, but at the same time acknowledging his printer's position.

"Just try to make Elizabeth's job as easy as possible," he'd say. "I know you have to concentrate on your work, but so does she. Co-operate on this. And if there is a problem – a serious problem – I want to know about it."

His efforts at conciliation were so sincere that we usually gave in and supressed the rage the secretary had aroused in us. At some moments we knew Mr. Goldberg was one of us, a printer from the past, a man trying to connect with his former skill, the trade he'd expected to spend the rest of his life working at. And very nearly succeeded.

The encounter with Elizabeth Begg had not helped my frustration with the machine. I stared at the parallel knives that trimmed each line as it emerged from the mold disk, as if staring at them would correct the problem. It was a difficult adjustment to make, and I needed Floyd badly. Fat and asthmatic, diabetic and aging badly, Floyd still knew the intimate workings of the Linotype better than anyone alive. He was always able to fix the machine when something serious went wrong with it. At such times I was reduced to primal helplessness, and the machine which I loved so dearly, became a dark, inert, mechanical *thing* – a beast of compassionless spitefulness that seemed to relish my state of despair. In this mood, I saw the machine as Felix Mason did: as just a machine, cranky, noisy, and dirty.

To the occasional visitor Mr. Goldberg showed through the shop, the Linotype must have seemed a strange device. It stood almost seven feet high, and jutted out from its base at curious, heavy angles. Even when I was not setting type, the machine moved continuously. Its several belts and pulleys running in different directions and at different speeds. Bright metal handles and wheels offered themselves in several positions on the machine. And if there was type in the steel galley near the keyboard, the visitor was always drawn to the shining lines that looked more like silver than lead.

At that point I would pick up one of the lines, and demonstrate the backwards letters on its face, and explain how the lines would be locked into a printing press, inked, and printed on paper. And I would explain how, until the last 25 or 30 years, the Linotype was the main tool used to set type for most books, magazines, and newspapers. If the visitor was over forty, I took pleasure in revealing that most of what he or she had read early in life was produced on a machine exactly like this one.

On the Linotype, I explained, words began as the customer's hand-written or typed copy, were filtered through the operator's sensory apparatus, and through the sinews of the body – the arms, wrists, fingers.

Once they spill off the ends of the fingers, I would explain, they enter the machine, assemble themselves in the brass matrices, forming words, and sentences. The machine seizes the brass words and take them into itself, where is does the hard, precise things to them.

The words, now in a line, descent into steel jaws – and I pointed these out to the visitor, who would peer cautiously into the machine – where the line is forcibly thrust against the mold face. Then the alchemical act occurs, the brief, violent process that is most similar to the human act, the human instant, of ejaculation.

A piston in the machine's hot crucible drives downward and spurts molten lead into the brass letters. It takes less than a second, a brief, hot climax, then it is over. The mold wheel, a twenty-inch steel disk, spins like a roulette wheel, a revolving mandala, then stops. The ejector blade forces the now solid, now hardened, but still hot, line of type out of the mold wheel and onto the steel tray, where it falls with a sharp clack.

The experienced operator can pick up the line, hot as it is, and read the words, upside-down and backwards. When the line is printed, of course, it all comes out right.

After I had given Kitty the tour, she stood looking at the machine, shaking her head.

"Why don't you tell the truth?" she said.

"What truth?"

"That a computer can do all of this in a fraction of the time and with better results."

"Can the computer have an orgasm?" I asked her.

"You'll have to take *my* tour and find out," she said.

When I finished the usual tour, Mr. Goldberg would thank me and lead the visitors away from the machine. Later, he would tell me I got too poetic again, that people don't give a damn about the machine as an alchemical wonder.

"They just don't appreciate it like we do," he'd say. "Try to keep it down to earth, keep it practical."

And I'd nod, yet I never felt chastised, because I knew Mr. Goldberg felt the same way I did, but just couldn't allow himself to express any outright enthusiasm. After what he'd been through, I didn't blame him.

CHAPTER TWO

It was more luck than skill that brought my type into alignment. I followed the instructions for adjusting the trimming knives given in a tattered 1040 copy of *Linotype Machine Principles,* and four times advanced the adjusting screws. After casting several test-lines I grew more and more frustrated and threw each handful of defective lines into the metal pot.

This was dangerous. Splashed lead sticks to the skin and burns while it cools. The surface of the molten lead sputtered, and two large drops of lead hit me in the face, one on the forehead, the other near my right eyebrow.

I cursed and knocked the already hardening flakes of metal off my skin, then went across the shop to the sink and splashed cold water onto the small burns.

"Eating lead again?" Felix Mason asked.

Mason was working on the Gardner press a few feet away, the huge cast iron flywheel revolving majestically at the side of the press.

"It's good," I said. "Want to try some?"

Mason laughed lightly, in his most irritating way. Beneath his laugh, I thought, was a contempt for anyone who didn't do his job well. But that might have been my imagination. I always felt that way after I'd been burned, as if the machine had punished me.

After the burns, however, the lines began to correct themselves. I patted the top of the first elevator, just as Mr. Goldberg had done.

"Thank you," I said. "Thank God and thank you – you beautiful old bitch."

I picked up ten lines from the machine's type tray, wincing because they were still quite hot, and took them to Harvey Wells, to show him the problem was corrected, and that I had corrected it myself. And to express my hurt and subdued anger at him for going over my head.

I did this, knowing in advance that Harvey wouldn't be impressed, and that he would find some other way to further infuriate me.

Harvey Wells occupied a middle ground, a central position in the shop. His domain, both figuratively and physically, mediated the worlds of type composition and printing production. Harvey took my type and assembled it into whatever format was required – pages, programs, advertisements, booklets, flyers, and catalogues. Harvey also did whatever hand composition was necessary, using the larger type that was kept in type cases stored in large wooden cabinets in his work area.

Harvey was also the stone man. And it was the stone that dominated the activity of the shop. The stone was a rectangular surface of machined iron, 51 inches by 73 inches, and 38 inches high. We knew the exact dimensions because we'd measured it 10 years before to make sure a new gas furnace could be brought into the shop and past Harvey's stone. There were two smaller stones in the shop, one at the back where Sam Storry ran the big Heidelberg cylinder press, and a very small stone on top of a cabinet in Harvey's work area. All of Harvey's jobs were locked up for the presses on the large metal stone. Supporting the stone was a frame with drawers for galleys and chases – steel frames that fit into the printing presses.

Harvey locked all the jobs into the chases with great skill and speed. I often held my breath as he lifted two columns of heavy Linotype material into the air, locked securely into position by wooden blocks and metal quoins. He often had time for short breaks and would stand at his stone with both palms pressed onto the flat, cool surface of the metal.

"Got it fixed up, did you?" he said, as I placed the bright lines on the stone.

"Feel them," I said.

"Looks good," he said, hefting in the lines. "The old clunker's acting up on you, is it?"

I nodded.

Mason joined us at the stone and lit a cigarette.

"Anyone for lunch?" he asked. He rested the heel of his palm on the stone, and flecks of ash fell onto the metal surface.

"Shit man," Harvey said. He brushed the ashes off the stone angrily.

"Get fucking real," Mason said calmly. I waited to see how Harvey, the oldest among the three of us, would react.

"Well goddamn it and real fuck to you too," he said. "It must be Friday, eh? Beer and shit sandwiches." He turned and moved away to his inclined job bank, where he began to bang spacing materials together.

"I guess he's coming," Mason grinned.

I shrugged. "It's Friday."

Mason chuckled. "Asshole." Mason pushed himself away from the stone and walked back to his press. I stood, feeling isolated and curiously upset. Goddamn and real fuck to both of you.

This was before the talented stone man nearly drowned on his holidays. Afterward he was a much-improved human being, but also a much stranger one. Mason believed that he was simply insane, and that if he hadn't been insane, he would have punched the old bugger right in his gold teeth.

Harvey Wells was in his early sixties, but lean and strong. His hair was going, and he had started to comb it across his skull. Yet he wasn't a vain man.

"You take I t as it comes, then you give it back," he often said, though after the near drowning he stopped saying it.

We learned just how close to the edge of nervous collapse Harvey was when the birds got into the shop. Galaxy Press was an old building, built in the downtown area before such one-story structures became impractical. Years before its wall had been broken at various places to attach wooden beams for a garage beside the building. The garage had long ago disappeared, to be replaced by a gravel parking lot. The holes and gaps in the brickwork were filled imperfectly, and became nesting places for birds, mostly sparrows.

We didn't know how deep the holes in the walls penetrated, until two sparrows suddenly emerged at the top of the interior wall and burst into the dingy air of the shop.

Harvey had just slid a locked-up job off the stone, and was headed for Mason's Heidelberg platen press, when the panicked birds swept over his head, wingtips brushing the top of his hair.

Harvey screamed and threw the form up in the air. When it hit the floor, it burst apart. Most of the type was hand-set and scattered like metal insects across the floorboards.

Harvey ran to the tiny washroom behind Mason's press and slammed the door shut. Mason began to laugh. I ducked and covered my head, fearful of the sudden eruption and wild rush of feathers in the shop.

The calmest person was the old man, Arnold Cleary, who was at the cutting machine at the rear of the shop. When the commotion started, Arnold looked up slowly, saw what was happening, and walked straight to the back door. He opened the door to the street and started to call to the birds. The birds by this time had started to fly against the windows. One already lay stunned on top of a bundle of paper stock.

Arnold went to the window and opened it. He picked up the injured bird and talked gently to it. The second bird flew over his shoulder and out the window. The bird in Arnold's calm hands began to revive and he lay it softly on the stone ledge outside the window.

Mr. Goldberg had come out of the office, his face registering alarm, his eyebrows raised curiously, as if he was about to cry.

"Where's Harvey?" he asked.

"He's hiding in the toilet bowl," Mason laughed.

Harvey didn't come out of the bathroom. He had climbed out the small window into the parking lot, and walked up the street, where he had coffee in a department store.

"They can kill you, you know," he said later, his expression serious. "Remember Hitchcock's film?"

When I arrived at Galaxy Press, Arnold Cleary was operating the old Gordon, and occasionally, the A.B. Dick offset press. When he wasn't working on these machines, he operated the cutting machine. I thought he was simply another pressman, nearing retirement. Eventually I discovered that there was much more to the man.

Arnold had, at one time, operated the Linotype machine at the Galaxy, had set type by hand, and had locked up forms on the stone whenever Harvey Wells was on holidays. When the pressman's union had finally managed to get enough members into the shop, they obliged Mr. Goldberg to sign a contract with the pressmen.

This, in turn, forced Arnold to choose between the pressroom and the comp room. He chose to be a pressman, though this made neither Arnold nor Mr. Goldberg particularly happy. Arnold moved from a position of being a total printer to being a pressman only, though certainly this was still a highly skilled trade in itself.

He was close to retirement in any case and took the new situation philosophically. Since he was able to perform other duties that fell within the pressman's job description, he was able to work on the cutting machine, and to visit customers, for consultation. No one could question whether or not he was, in fact, running errands.

Other minor jobs came his way, and Arnold actually enjoyed the release from the daily production schedules a pressman faced. Someone in the shop – Felix Mason believed it was Sam Storry – reported this to the union, causing a slight disturbance for both Arnold and Mr. Goldberg. The local union, however, was flexible, and allowed one of its members to perform what would normally be considered an apprentice's duties, as long as Arnold received a journeyman's pay.

My own union, however, jealously guarded its rapidly fading authority. Herb Dennett, the local secretary, visited me at the shop, once, to advise me on the matter.

I had thought that it was only at union meetings that officers of the local became strangely sweaty and wore the odd clothing of unionists – checkered shirts and cheap trousers; but Dennett's face looked greasy even in the light from the windows as he stood beside me, in front of my machine. He wore a short-sleeved shirt with a Black Watch pattern, and his pants were creaseless, as if he, or his wife, had forgotten to iron them.

"The old man isn't doing anything he isn't supposed to, is he?"

"What old man?"

I didn't particularly like Dennett. Like so many of his kind, the supposed power of the union touched and inflated a weak area of his psyche. It was the same area that caused some unionists to swear at meetings with management, and to pretend they owned the employees, if not the company.

"Cleary," Dennett said, glanding down the shop.

I should my head. "No. Just what he's supposed to be doing."

Dennett didn't seem satisfied with the answer but nodded anyway. The days of the I.T.U.'s hegemony were, at that time, rapidly diminishing; and it was difficult for people like Dennett to accept the new situation. As difficult as it was for me to admit my machine was being replaced with a new process, and that my trade was drying up inside me, like nerve endings that no longer sensed the outside world, and retreated slowly into darkness.

Arnold was intelligent and looked intelligent. His white hair was quite long, and he combed it back over the sides, in what used to be called a ducktail in the fifties. He was slender, but fairly strong for a man in his sixties. He knew how to pace himself, and he rarely become angry. Nor did he swear.

On breaks, or at lunch, he spoke knowledgeably about what was happening in the world, drawing most of his information from the newspapers and Maclean's magazine. But like most printers, myself included, his knowledge was not deep, nor supported by a disciplined education. Great ideas were often given to us to put into print, but little of it stayed with us, just as a stone mason may lay bricks into a magnificent building, yet not comprehend the soaring architecture he is bringing into being. The stone mason, however, like the printer, can look at the finished product, and say, with very real pride, "I did that."

If between them Herb Dennett and Arnold Cleary had produced a newly-printed edition of the Bible, Arnold's pride would have been acceptable and understandable; Dennett's pride, emerging through his oily face and Black Watch shirt would have merely aroused disbelief, and possibly contempt.

CHAPTER THREE

"Just what do you think you are doing there?" Kitty asked me once, in exasperation.

Kitty was on an electronic high that evening. When she opened her apartment door I could see at once that she was aroused and excited. Her face was flushed and her hair in disarray. Her eyes were wide, almost popping, and a slight sheen of perspiration glistened on her throat. Instinctively, I feared the worst – that she had another lover, and that she had just got up from her brass bed, hastily arranged her clothes, and run to open the door.

"Come in," she said breathlessly. She grabbed my shirt and tugged me through the door, kissing me simultaneously.

"What's going on?" I asked. "Is someone here?" Kitty was almost as tall as me. She cocked her head and looked directly into my eyes.

"What someone?" She was genuinely puzzled, and my fears subsided. It was the same fear, the same rush of disequilibrium I had felt when Clare had told me about her lover, and her plans for departure.

"Look, look," Kitty said, tugging me into the living room. She pointed towards the kitchen table, where her computer occupied the area in front of large windows looking out on the balcony ten stories above the ground. The computer screen was on, and a column of curious symbols floated motionless on the green-tinted background. "Sea-green," she'd told me. "I prefer water imagery – the sea, or better – a great river, a flowing Nile of information. I've just come out of it," she said, urging me even closer to the screen. "I've been in the stream, in the ocean."

"Please," I said, letting her feel my body slump. "I came here for sex, not to dive into your computer soup-bowl." The body-slump had its effect. She nodded and took a few deep breaths.

"I need a break anyway," she said. "Wait till I tell you where I've been."
I dropped into the softness of her Naugahyde couch.

"There should be a few beers left," I said.

"There is. I've got to shut this down – go get us a couple." She shut off
the monitor, and I sighed audibly as the screen went blank. We faced each
other on the couch, our knees almost touching.

"Give me hot metal any day," I said.

Kitty smiled. "They used to pour hot lead on attacking enemies," she
said.

"What's that got to do with anything?"

"Now they've got smart bombs." She thought she had won her point.

"Both were meant for killing people," I said lamely.

"That's beside the point," she said. "Try fighting a war today with hot
lead."

"There's another kind of hot lead," I said. But she wasn't to be turned
aside. I had set myself up, and now I had to be knocked down.

"Just what is it you think you are doing there?"

I pretended to think. "Taking words and giving them substance," I
said. "Turning language into something you can touch, feel, hold in your
hand."

Kitty laughed loudly. "But words come from the brain from electrical
activity. For the first time in history, the writing tool is the extension of
the mind."

"It always has been," I said. "Feel it."

She laughed, "you pathetic jerk."

Kitty was right, of course, there really was no defence for Galaxy Press,
or for any of us who continued to work there. We were like religious groups
who maintain their old ways, driving horse-drawn buggies on roads built
for fast-moving cars, and in a world where highways are built entirely of
electronic signals.

Yet, like religious revisionists, the product we produced was essentially
the same as the output of the high-tech industries. The faithful farmers
planted, nurtured, and harvested their crops, then sold the produce to a
greedy public who were amused at their simplicity.

Customers who came to Galaxy Press had to wait longer to get their
business cards, wedding invitations, programs, books, and advertising

material, but what they received was printed with skills equal to most of what was produced by often unskilled keyboard operators. The digital crowd, we called them, when we referred to them at all.

Yet not one of us at the Galaxy thought we were going to survive those who had replaced us. What we had, and what we knew was that we were skilled tradesmen, who were good at what we did.

Perversely, someone always highlighted the latest innovation from copies of *The Globe and Mail or The Toronto Star* that were brought into the shop.

"Look at this," Harvey said, during a break, holding the newspaper out at arm's length, as if to check the alignment of the columns.

"Now someone's found a way for people to check out their own groceries. *Hah!*"

He looked over the top of the pater at whoever was listening.

"Completely does away with checkout clerks," he said, biting off each word for emphasis.

"Bastards," Mason said with practiced contempt.

"Someone, somewhere," Arnold Cleary said, "thought hard how to replace human workers. That's a pretty sad thing."

And Arnold *looked* sad, as if he were worn out from seeing such things. And of course, he had seen a lot. In his 70-odd years of life, he was fond of telling us, he had seen a great deal.

According to Arnold, he became conscious of the wider world at age 10. If there was time, and if anyone seemed interested, he would enumerate the changes of the Twentieth Century he saw as they occurred.

"I personally remember the invention of the electron microscope, the tape recorder, the development of penicillin, and..." he paused significantly, "the first electronic computer, in 1941. I remember the invention of the transistor, the polio vaccine. Television, of course."

And he would go on until someone stopped him. If he missed something, one of us would announce the omission proudly, as if to prove he was a bonafide member of the century, someone who had been there when it happened. Often this would be something silly, and it was usually Harvey who came up with it.

"The invention of the shopping cart!" he'd yell. "The food blender, the cigarette filter, the wireless coat hanger!"

"The biggest inventions were not designed to replace people," Arnold once told us. They were designed to kill people. Nuclear weapons – ICBMs, the cruise missile, the smart-bombs, the biological and nerve gases."

"And a machine to replace thinking," I added, but with so little enthusiasm no one noticed.

Arnold's statement was unprovable and went unchallenged since we usually lacked the time for a lengthy discussion. But at the Galaxy not everyone agreed on everything all of the time. Sam Storry, though he seldom contributed anything, was subversive in ways that were unexpected and disliked by the rest of us.

"You comps have already been replaced," he said, after Felix Mason read something from the *Globe* about the disappearance of the book.

His statement was directed at Harvey Wells and me, the only compositors at the Galaxy.

Harvey snorted, and began pinching his arms. "I must be imagining myself then," he chortled.

"A disk this size," Sam made one corner of a square with his thumb and forefinger, "can hold the information for a whole book – including page sizes, type, borders, everything."

"Tell us something new," I said. "What's your point?"

Sam shrugged and smirked. "How's it feel to be replaced by a piece of plastic?"

"How will it feel when we stick your head into the Heidelberg?" Harvey said seriously.

What Sam said, of course, was true. But at Galaxy Press it was a sacrilege to say it, just as it would be a sacrilege – and pointless – to tell a Mennonite carriage maker that both he and his horses had been replaced by a piston engine the size of a bushel basket.

There were days in that last year when time seemed to collapse on itself, and events occurred that would normally have taken much longer to develop on their own. As they did in the period before the Linotype's appearance in 1886, when news had to wait to happen, to give newspapers time to typeset and print the stories. One of the collapsed days was early in the summer. It was Harvey's last day before his holidays, and a week before his drowning. It was the day Mason brought Kitty to our Friday pub lunch. And it was the day Sam Storry announced he was leaving Galaxy Press – the first real sign that the end of the Galaxy was upon us.

There was no particular reason the four of us should have drunk together. Mason and I got along reasonably well, but Harvey was difficult to talk to in the outside world as he was locking up type on his stone.

Sam Storry, the pressman, was the least sociable of all of us. He was a strange, quiet man who was born into awkwardness. His body hung together at curious angles, and his hair never seemed to sit comfortably on his scalp, no matter how much gel he plastered on it. Mason cruelly dubbed him Cowlick and called Sam this to his face.

But Sam was no fool. He did his job well enough. He not only operated the Heidelberg cylinder press at the back of the shop, he also did all the offset jobs that came in. the small offset press, old as it was, was the only piece of equipment at Galaxy Press that could be said to belong to new era printing. Mr. Goldberg had shrugged at this single inconsistency in his shop.

"It helps keep us going," he said once, as Sam Storry and Mason struggled with one of the machine's frequent breakdowns. "At least it pays the water bill."

Sam didn't talk much, nor did he seem to listen very much. Like many printers, he was poor company. We were, however, all printers, and there was something important and necessary about drinking together. If the great American printer, Benjamin Franklin, had worked at Galaxy Press, he would be admonishing us, as he did his own journeymen, not to drink too much at noon, to remain bright and clear-headed for the afternoon's work. We frequently toasted Ben Franklin with our last beer at lunch. All except Sam Storry, who simply shifted his lumpy, awkward body in his chair and looked sourly at the phoney surroundings of the Queen's Inn. It was supposed to resemble a royal court, with its stained murals of a fat, pompous queen, and various hangers-on. Some sort of clown performed tricks below the queen's feet, at the level of the tabletop pushed against the wall. The draught at the Queen's Inn, however, was fine, and the hot ham sandwiches helped to clear the printing dust and chemicals from our palates.

Mason was 10 minutes late. When he came into the pub, he had Kitty Travis with him. She looked out of place in the tavern. The lunch-time crowd turned in the gloom to watch her as she and mason came to our table.

"Gentlemen, this is Kitty Travis. Eat out your hearts. Kitty, these are the printers." Kitty smiled down at us, brightly, and not in the least condescendingly. She wore pink and blue that day, and the colours contrasted strangely with the washed-out blue of the murals on the walls around her. The fat grotesque queen stared down at Kitty, who was slender, cool, and beautiful. Mason and Kitty sat down. The resentment soon became palpable. No woman had ever joined us at the Queen's Inn.

"Kitty is totally new era," Mason said, as if proud of himself.

"What era is that?" Harvey said, addressing Kitty.

She smiled at Harvey, interested by the obstinate tone of his voice.

"Felix tells me you all use old equipment – no computers."

"Ha!" Harvey laughed suddenly, startling Kitty. Then he did it again. "*Ha!*"

"I'm going to bring her in to see the place," Mason said. "She can't believe it exists." Mason glanced at Kitty, and in the casual flicker of his eyes over her face and upper torso, there was the confidence of arrogant self-assurance. You bastard, I thought. What exactly could a woman like this see in an inflated pressman who vaguely resembled Frank Sinatra in middle age? Mixed with the irritation of her presence, was the pain and envy, and the instant self-pity that envy pours into the heart. At least in my heart.

"You'd better wear something different," Sam Storry said suddenly, leaning towards Kitty. "It's pretty dirty in the shop."

Mason laughed. "I've already told her how dirty printers are."

Kitty smiled, going along with the banter. Her eyes stopped at me, and she regarded me frankly.

"They don't look so dirty to me," she said.

"Him especially," Mason chortled. "Watch the fingers – he dabbles on keyboards."

Ignorant pressman, I thought.

Harvey raised his beer glass into the air. "A toast to the lady," he said loudly and inappropriately. Heads turned in the gloom again. We drank to Kitty, and Kitty drank to herself, amused.

"We have to go," Mason said, rising.

Kitty stood up behind him. Mason stuck his hand in front of Harvey's face.

"You're off next week?"

Harvey frowned and nodded, then quickly shook Mason's hand.

"For two weeks," he said. "Heavy thinking, drinking, swimming."

"You're not coming back to the shop?" I asked Mason.

"I'm sick this afternoon," he said seriously. "My cousin here is taking me home."

He looked at Kitty who, to her credit, didn't smile. They turned and left the pub. Heads moved.

"I'll be going too," Sam Storry said.

Harvey looked sharply at the pressman.

"Say again?"

This was Harvey's most recent linguistic acquisition, and his most unpleasant. He tried on new expressions in some sort of attempt to keep up with his mind's disconnected flow. I thought of Professor James' thesis about word.

Sam Storry leaned forward on the table and looked – for the first time since I'd known him – as if he were being intimate. As if he wanted to share something of himself with us.

"You're sick too?" Harvey asked.

Sam shook his head.

"No. I'm going to quit. Work someplace else."

For several moments both Harvey and I were silent. This was nothing new to any of us, of course. Printers, like most tradesmen, were always coming and going, that's why they were originally called journeymen. But no one had come or gone at Galaxy Press for at least five years, since Mason arrived.

"The place is going to fold pretty soon," Sam said. "We all know that."

Harvey snorted. "We all know we're gonna die someday – so what?"

"So, what are you going to do?" Sam said, louder than necessary. "Where are you gonna work? Who needs a *stone* man these days?" Harvey and I were surprised and a little amused. Sam rarely got aroused enough about anything to raise his voice.

"At least I can run an offset press," Sam said. "And I'm going to work for a place where that's *all* they have."

"What you run is not an offset press," Harvey said. "It's a goddamned sheet-choker, a piss-pot whoop-de-shit!"

When Harvey tried to invent new descriptive words, he began to spit and stutter.

"A *whoop-de-shit?*" I asked.

"Anyway," Sam Storry said, "I'm tired of working for that bloody Jew."

That was his parting comment. He got up and walked awkwardly out of the pub.

Harry glanced at his watch.

"We're late," he said, though he made no effort to move.

"I didn't know he was anti-Semitic," I said.

Harvey sneered at me. "If the old man was an atheist, he'd hate atheists."

"Harvey," I said, but then hesitated.

"What? Let's go."

"Are you really going to go swimming?"

"You think I'm too old?" He thrust his leg out beyond the table. "Feel that muscle. I may be half a century old, but that is not flab at all. Go on, feel it."

I didn't touch his leg. We stood up and left the pub.

I was thirteen when I learned about the Holocaust. Like many teenagers, I was morbidly interested in violent death of any sort, was drawn to war – which I knew little about – as if it lay just under the ground, exerting a black, tidal pull on the daylight world of the sixties. My introversion absorbed the new horrors I discovered like a psychic blotter. Books were easy enough to find, and photographs of human bodies being bulldozed into mass graves had a dizzying, almost stupefying effect on my adolescent sensibilities. The only thing more overpowering in my life at that time was the effects of sexuality, and its availability to a powerful, inwardly directed will.

For a long period, perhaps two years, I did not know what to do with the revelations of the Holocaust. I was too young to be able to connect it to the apocalyptic images of the Bible or see it with anything close to an adult's mature horror and disbelief. There were not even any of the despicable revisionists, so common in later years, where my overwhelmed consciousness might have found an easily available target.

Much later, when I came to work for Galaxy Press, I was pleased to find myself working for Mr. Goldberg. By then, however, I had lost my youthful enthusiasm for opening the pit of the Holocaust at the slightest opportunity. It was nonetheless a revelation to discover that Mr. Goldberg wad a survivor of a concentration camp. When I was told, I tried very hard – until I succeeded after several months – to see the tattooed number on Mr., Goldberg's arm.

It was a particularly hot summer day, and all of us were helping bring in large bundles of paper for an unusually big job for the rotary press. Mr. Goldberg was quickly winded and was sweating profusely. We made him rest, and he leaned against Harvey's stone and unbuttoned his shirt sleeves.

Arnold Cleary talked to the boss to make sure he was all right. Then I saw Mr. Goldberg pull up his shirt sleeves, one after the other. I dropped my bundle of paper and hurried to the stone.

"We're almost finished," I told him, staring at his arms. I saw the tattoo and was surprised how insignificant it looked.

I had to wait another year before Arnie told me what I thought I should know, and felt I almost had a right to know – what had happened to Mr. Goldberg during the war.

It was a brief story yet surpassed the human tragedy I had been used to contemplating. Mr. Goldberg had been an apprentice in his uncle's printing company in Lodz, Poland, in the mid-thirties. It was expected that he would learn all there was to know about the trade, then move into a management position in the shop – which was called Droga Mleczna. Galaxy Press.

The Holocaust intervened. Mr. Goldberg's family lost the company as well as their homes and possessions, and ultimately their lives. Most of the family perished – all except Mr. Goldberg and his sister Rose, who survived and reached North America after the war.

His sister had managed to take some of the family's resources with her, converted into precious stones. When they were reunited in 1950, she and Mr. Goldberg used most of the family's wealth to start Galaxy Press back to life. Rose saw her brother turn the company into a close replica of the gloomy shop they had known in their youth in Lodz.

Rose died of pancreatic cancer before the printing industry began to transform itself, before printing shops began to resemble something new, and foreign, something painful to behold.

Mr. Goldberg, however, maintained the illusion of Droga Mleczna. He must have hoped he would die before he had to close Galaxy Press, or before he had to transfer it into something that didn't resemble itself.

All the time I worked at the Galaxy, I knew about the Holocaust book Mr. Goldberg had printed. A man he had known in Poland had come to him with a manuscript of recollections about his life in Poland during the German occupation, and the expulsion of the Jews.

The man was older than Mr. Goldberg and had been an adult when Mr. Goldberg met him in Lodz. Through a newspaper story they had found each other in this part of the world. The man, Jacob Rosen, had been a baker in Lodz, and was delighted that Mr. Goldberg had continued his family's printing company in Canada. And very quickly Rosen produced a sheaf of hand-written notes about his experiences during the war.

Mr. Goldberg agreed to print Rosen's notes as a memoir, without cost to Rosen, who operated a modest bakery at the edge of a Jewish neighbourhood near the city's downtown core. According to Arnold Cleary, they printed only two hundred copies, which Jacob Rosen distributed to friends and family members. A few copies were carried in local bookstores, but it was never Rosen's intention to make money on the book, or to see recognition for it.

A few copies remained at Galaxy Press. One was kept in the office at all times, on a shelf along with other work the Galaxy had produced over the years. Another copy was somewhere in the basement, and a third copy circulated around the shop in a curious, peripatetic passage from place to place, and hand to hand.

I first saw it in Harveys area, laying on the granite stone of a cabinet containing cases of miscellaneous typefaces and designs. A year later it found its way to the back table near the flatbed press. There, during lunch and work breaks, it was occasionally picked up, read briefly, commented on, then casually placed back, on the table. Its title did not encourage interest. *Shoah* meant nothing to any of us, and wouldn't until the film *Schindler's List* brought the reality of the Holocaust back to the forgetful consciousness of our aging century.

Sam Storry treated the book with contempt.

"It wasn't six million. That's crap."

"How many was it?" Arnold Cleary asked him.

"Maybe a million," Sam said, shrugging, obviously not interested enough to debate the subject.

Arnold Cleary shook his head.

"Only a million?" he said.

Sam looked away, as he usually did when speaking directly to anyone. He picked up a loose page of the newspaper and began to study it.

Sometime in the next two years *Shoah* progressed to the front of the shop, where if found an uneasy position beside a stack of specialty paper in a steel cabinet. I picked it up from there and brought it to the Linotype section, where it had begun its printing history. I kept it safely on the top shelf of my wooden tool and parts cabinet.

Gradually, over time, I read most of the book. None of it surprised me, but because it was connected to the Galaxy in a particularly personal way, it had a substance that other books did not. There were two references to Drukarnia Galaktyka in the book.

Rosen wrote that he had visited the shop in Lodz to order handbills, and described its musty, chemically-strong atmosphere – its dust, its noise, its ink smudges. He managed to convey the essence of all print shops everywhere. Certainly, he accurately described the Drukarnia Galaktyka as it must have been.

The second mention of the company was probably added later, to make Mr. Goldberg happy. Rosen described the workers in greater detail, especially one young apprentice who seemed to do nothing but sweep the floor.

"He was a serious young fellow, who performed his single work with enthusiasm and thoroughness. Later I found out that this was the owner's son, Simon. He was to become a master printer in time, but did not know that time was soon going to end for all of us. This young man in another world was to be my dear friend and fellow in hardship."

The prose was inelegant, but I was touched by the simple recollection of Rosen's immense pain and sorrow. When he wrote about the disappearance of his wife into Treblinka, I felt a bizarre kinship of loss with him, sensed his terrifying, total abandonment.

Once, as an experiment, I typeset the word *shoah,* then picked the brass letters from the assembler and held them between my fingers. For this first time I sensed how the metal could be stained by the meaning of the words they formed. Like the gold in the teeth of *shoah's* victims, the brass was transmuted into glittering metaphors of death, the hollow indentation of each tiny letter-mold a mass grave of meaning...

CHAPTER FOUR

The discovery of the tombstone in the shop was one of the more phenomenal events of the Galaxy's history. For the remainder of our time together, we amused ourselves with the wonderful significance of what we had found. It was appropriate that we found it in Harvey's work area. After his return to work, and after his drowning, Harvey had changed in many ways. Some changes were very subtle, and some revealed more profound and inexplicable personality shifts. Harvey had always been meticulous about his surroundings. In his 25 years at Galaxy Press he had arranged his part of the shop the way he wanted it, and he exercised absolute control over his small domain. His job bank, with its inclined surface, was only three feet from the make-up stone. He needed only to turn, with the galley in his hand, and take two steps to the stone. Even the galley was special to him. It was made of solid brass and was almost as wide as it was long. Whenever he found himself with a few free moments – which had become more frequent towards the end – he would get out his can of Brasso and start polishing the galley. It always shone with a rich, deep glow, and Harvey often stood the galley on its end and combed his thin hair in its rippled surface.

To use the galley, he simply laid its edge on the edge of the stone and slid the work onto the stone's smooth surface. The work was always tied securely with string so it wouldn't fall apart as it slipped from the polished brass onto the machined iron. The cabinets containing the type Harvey used most frequently were aligned with his bank, so that he simply walked up and down in front of the cabinets with his composing stick in his hand. The stick, like the tone, was made of metal, and carried the name of the material from which, historically, it had been made. The type fonts in the cabinets were the usual display faces, each individual drawer in the cabinet holding a different size type. In one cabinet he kept all his gothic faces

– Helvetica, Kabel, Twentieth-Century Gothic, and Universe. The scripts were also kept together, in the same cabinet as Old English and Wedding Text. At the end of the row were the standard roman fonts – a complete family of Times Roman, including bold and italic fonts, in five different sizes. Here too were the older faces – Garamond Caslon and Bodoni. Even the names of these types were beautiful. Once printed onto good stock, the graceful strokes, curves, and serifs of the type move elegantly to a place in the printer's mind that is reserved for this kind of beauty and nothing else. Perhaps it is a typographic gene, an inborn sensibility inherited from the scribes who originated many of the designs when all reproduction was done by hand. This is one area of the trade where Harvey and I agreed completely. In fact, I never met a compositor who wasn't emotionally moved by the type with which he worked. We weren't designers, but we loved the materials of our craft, and we were connected in a way we didn't understand to everyone who had worked in the craft before us, all the way back to Johan Gutenberg. I had some of the same typefaces on my machine, each stored in a separate magazine. But mind were the smaller sizes, which were used for texts too long to be set by hand. The sizes I worked with ranged from six-point to twelve-point. Farther away from Harvey, and around the corner, were the typefaces that had been popular in the twenties and thirties, had fallen into disuse, and then came back into style in the eighties and nineties, when many people excitedly thought they were entirely new designs created just for them. In the last cabinet, and the one farthest from Harvey's bank, were the type cases containing an assortment of odds and ends. Some cases held nothing but esoteric border pieces, and small engravings showing twenties-style cartoon figures doing a number of commercial tasks – answering phones, typing letters, delivering telegrams on bicycles, or waving from the decks of cruise ships riding on stylized waves. It was the top of this last cabinet that held and concealed the tombstone.

Soon after his return, Harvey decided that the symmetry of his world must be dismantled – to match, presumably, some mysterious, interior change in his psyche. Harvey asked for help to arrange his work area into a large semi-circle. All the type cabinets were to be positioned to form an arc that was to be as geometrically accurate as possible.

"From now on," he said grandly, "there are to be no corners."

"Hundervasser," Arnold Cleary said.

"What's that?" Harvey said, pausing, his arms still forming a descriptive arc in the air.

The old man shrugged. "The artist – Hundervasser. He said there are no straight lines in nature."

"And I say there are no corners," Harvey said.

Mr. Goldberg listened to Harvey's plan, but shook his head doubtfully. He pointed out, correctly, that such an arc would waste valuable floor space. I expected Harvey to waggle his head say something ridiculous like "Woe-be-damned space, you say!" But he didn't. This was the new Harvey, the Harvey who had drowned and returned from death.

"Yes, I see that," he said, with obvious respect in his voice. "We can make the arc more shallow. But *that* will have to go."

He had quickly moved through his area, as if on skates, his finger pointing accusingly as the old cabinet with its marble top.

Mr. Goldberg shrugged slowly. He was much weaker by his time, and resignation dragged at his shoulders and back with noticeable effects.

A number of tools were kept in a closet at the back of the shop, near the cylinder press – a large crowbar, a six-foot moving bar, a scarred claw hammer, a five-pound ball-peen hammer, a saw and various battered and bent screwdrivers. We armed ourselves with these tools and started to work on the cabinet. We stack the drawers on top of each other near the shelves of paper stock. Mason pried at the wood trim holding the stone in place. The wood was destroyed by dry-rot, and popped away from its nails with short, loud shrieks.

"Okay, let's lift the sucker off," Harvey said. The rest of us stood back a few feet to give Harvey room to maneuver. He seized the marble top with both hands and lifted it. The stone was not as thick as we expected it would be, and Harvey was able to lift it out of the wooden frame easily, though his arms were trembling. Mason moved in to take one end of the stone, and the two of them lowered it to the floor.

"Great bejeczuz shit," Harvey said, abruptly returning to his old state of sudden alarm. "Look at this beauty!" The other side of the marble stone was engraved with weather-worn letters and numbers.

"It's a tombstone," Arnold Cleary said, wiping his hands together, though he hadn't touched anything. Mr. Goldberg joined the small group of suddenly quiet printers.

"What is it?" he asked, bending to look at the words.

"Lift it up," Mason said. "So we can see it better." Harvey and Felix Mason returned the tombstone to the top of the cabinet and stood it on its bottom end. It had been trimmed so that it was rectangular and could be put to a use for which it was never intended. Arnold Cleary adjusted his glasses and read the inscription.

JEREMY MILLER

1835 – 1899

beloved husband, father, grandfather
Of life's three burdens, "Change, Loss, and Sorrow"
He knew each intimately

"A tombstone," Sam Storry said.

Mr. Goldberg touched the letters with his fingers, savouring, as we all did, the mystery of its presence in the shop.

We spent some minutes studying the tombstone and conjecturing about how it came to be where we had found it, and where the actual remains of Jeremy Miller might lie.

"He might be under us," Mason said.

It seemed reasonable. The building may have been built over Miller's grave. But if that was true, his body would have been disturbed, for directly below us was the eight-foot-deep basement with its concrete floor.

"Maybe the rats ate him," Arnold Cleary said.

Harvey finally got us back to work, returning us to his vision of a large arc created from type cabinets and the imagination of a man who had undergone some sort of sea-change.

Mason told us later that he did not go home at exactly four o'clock that day. He was finishing up a rush-job and was the last printer to leave the building. Mr. Goldberg, of course, was still there. He always stayed alone in the shop, frequently moving quietly among the machines and type, without apparent purpose. I suspected that in his mind he was moving through the print shop in Lodz, Poland, and that in the semi-gloom of late afternoon he was again 14 years old with a good future ahead of him. Mason had finished washing up, and hearing nothing in the shop, looked around for Mr. Goldberg. He moved to Harvey's newly arced area, and heard a weak, hiccupping sound. The tombstone had been leaned against the drawers that we had removed from the cabinet. Mr. Goldberg was sitting on a paper bundle and had one arm over the top of the tombstone. He was crying quietly.

CHAPTER FIVE

Kitty was a woman of the nineties, although even now I don't fully understand what is meant by that term. There were a few common features that were facts of life, but there was no way a man could talk sensibly about women during that time, and even today it remains a difficult, and to some extent, a foolish undertaking. In twenty-two years of marriage, I had never learned to talk to my wife. When the time approached for our marriage to end, it was she who pointed out what happened. She had read about it in a still popular book on the subject. She did not shirk from the pain involved in recognizing the loss of what had initially been strong and – I had thought – durable. But marriages, she instructed me, like governments and business institutions, were in a process of transformation. And, of course, she had a new lover. The nature of pain and loss, however, hadn't kept up with the transformed reality. Sorrow was not yet computerized. And no one had taught me how to hot-wire my nervous system, how to connect it to the electronic river that was rushing towards the Ocean of Thought, as one pundit put it. Even Professor James could offer me little solace when I needed it. For me it was safer to remain in the world of hot lead, and noisy machines, to wrestle with obstinate, but easily understandable difficulties.

At the other end of the nineties' definition were women like Kitty. She was aggressive, not assertive. She was easily equal to any man in self-confidence, ambition, and ability and it was partly this strong sense of being that attracted me to her in the beginning. Perhaps I wanted to be mothered, and even punished, if I stepped out of line. I might have yearned to be told, as I was occasionally told by early female teachers, that I counted for something, that I was a worthy human being. I might even – at times – have wanted to be loved. Kitty was capable of all these things, and more. When she first came to visit Mason at the shop, she came through the 'NO

ADMITTANCE' door into the shop itself, ignoring the clearly marked office entrance. I was skimming the surface of the lead pot when she came in. She waved at me, and I instinctively responded. The skimming spoon was in my hand, and I raised it awkwardly in the air, small drops of lead fell onto my knuckles and burned there – tiny, intense spots of pain. Kitty moved past the sink, towards Mason, who was at the Heidelberg platen press, with his back to her. She wore a subdued outfit, a black skirt, and an ultramarine silk blouse. She walked gracefully and confidently through the grime and the dingy air, as if she were perfectly at ease in a print shop – and probably was. I sat down in front of the keyboard. I had only one job at the time, and I knew I could finish it within an hour. Then I would have to consult with Elizabeth Begg to avoid a major debate over new meanings for "miscellaneous". The work, like Galaxy Press, was drying up. By raising myself slightly in my chair I could watch Kitty as she talked to Mason. They were the same height, a fact which made Kitty seem taller than she was. Mason turned and leaned his forearm on the rectangular safety guard of the Heidelberg. He smiled as he talked to Kitty and took something from her hand and looked at it – a photograph, no doubt. I was envious. Again, I could see nothing in Mason that would attract a woman like Kitty to him. Yet even in his late forties, Mason enjoyed an inexplicable success with women. It is a mystery that has troubled me throughout my life. Why had Gertie Fleming, in grade two, ignored my passionate interest in her and followed the idiotic class fool, Jaimie Lewis? Why had Clare left me for a foot doctor with bad breath?

Mr. Goldberg came out of the office, with a customer beside him. He paused to gesture at Mason's press, and Mason glanced at Mr. Goldberg guiltily. Kitty smiled warmly, and even from across the shop, and from behind my machine, her smile stunned me. I could tell, by the way he stood, that Mr. Goldberg was confused by Kitty's presence in the shop. Visits from the printers' families and friends were rare, and though tolerated, they were not encouraged. When Mr. Goldberg disapproved of something, it appeared in his posture as a slight stiffness. Now, as he regarded Kitty and Mason, both confusion and disapproval were manifested in his thick, soft body. Kitty must have seen this, for she immediately made small preparatory movements to show that she was about to leave. Within seconds she lightly kissed Mason on the cheek and left the shop smoothly.

Beautifully. Mr. Goldberg moved closer to Mason and his press, obviously beginning a short tour for the customer. They would pass through the press room side of the shop, linger at Harvey's stone, then come over to my area, the Linotype department. The visitor, who was clearly a new customer, was a curious figure. He was perhaps five years younger than Mr. Goldberg, and slightly taller, but there was something insignificant about him. His clothes were neatly pressed but hung loosely on his body. He had a thick grey beard, that he continuously pushed down towards his neck, so that he looked like a strutting bird, bobbing its head. The two of them, walking down the centre of the shop, reminded me of old comedians from the early twenties. Mr. Goldberg actually walked a little like Charlie Chaplin, and the visitor could easily have passed for Buster Keaton, with a beard. They arrived, at last, in my area. I began to change the settings on the machine, both to look busy and to impress the visitor. There were six basics settings on the machine, and to change them all meant manipulating six entirely different mechanisms on the machine. An observer had the impression that the operator was involved in an intensely complicated activity, hands moving smoothly and rapidly across the front of the machine. They waited until I had finished, the Mr. Goldberg stepped forward, smiling.

"This is Mr. Evans," Mr. Goldberg said. Then, turning to Mr. Evans, he introduced me. "This is the Typesetter," he said. "He is the man who is going to put your book into type."

Mr. Evans was appropriately impressed and thrust out his hand. I shook it, noticing the thick manila envelope under his left arm. Mr. Evans pushed his beard downward, and I thought he was about to say something, but he merely raised his chin, as if to show me another view of his beard.

"I expect you will be meeting occasionally," Mr. Goldberg said. "To iron out any problems. Once you start to get your proofs you may want to talk to the typesetter to resolve any problems of style."

I was still sitting in my green Linotype chair. "What kind of job is it?" I asked, looking at the envelope.

"This is a novel," Mr. Evans said, his arm tightening over the envelope so that it made a crackling sound.

I was relieved. That meant straight-forward typesetting. Straight matter, the best and easiest kind of typesetting.

"I'll have a docket made up and bring it out when it's ready," Mr. Goldberg said to me.

"What type do you want me to use?" I asked both of them.

There was an intensity in Evans' face I hadn't noticed at first. He was obviously a highly stressed individual and seemed awkward and shy. I wondered if he would be able to relinquish his manuscript so I could typeset it. Mr. Goldberg looked at Evans and raised his eyebrows. Evans pushed his beard down and said nothing.

"We'll look at the type samples," Mr. Goldberg said. "Mr. Evans can choose from them." I nodded and put out my hand. Evans struggled briefly with the package under his arm, then stuck out his other hand, and we shook.

"Thank you," he said. "I will likely have a lot of things to talk to you about." His voice was taut, almost fearful.

It was not going to be pleasant working with Evans. He could easily have been Elizabeth Begg's brother. The two men left, and I changed the settings on my machine again. The choice of typeface was important. Unlike computers, once you chose a typeface on the Linotype, you were stuck with it. If the customer wanted to change the type halfway through the book, everything had to be reset in lead. Solid, heavy beautiful lead.

The customer's full name was Wynford Myers Evans. He was publishing his own novel. We occasionally had customers who were frustrated in their attempts to get published, and finally resorted to their last hope for seeing their work in print – self publication. It was odd, however, that Wynford Evans came to Galaxy Press. He could have typeset the manuscript himself on a computer that would not have cost much more than he was paying to have me do it. On top of this was the cost of printing and binding the book, although this would have been about the same no matter where it was done. But Mr. Goldberg was an honourable man, and I knew he had explained these things to Evans. Mr. Evans, I soon discovered, had his own reasons for coming to Galaxy Press. He wanted his book typeset in lead. The *prima materia*. An important alchemical substance in his mind, apparently, since it was somewhat related to the themes of his novel.

The manuscript came to me the next day, re-packaged in one of the larger docket envelopes, complete with a set of time sheets. I removed the manuscript, immediately recognizing the feel of corrigible bond. Mr.

Evans, like me, belonged to another time period. I lifted off the title page of the novel and placed it on the table behind my machine. The words were hand-printed in a poor imitation of type.

The Odyssey of
Adam Rice

[A modern Lazarus]
by

WYNFORD MYERS EVANS

One of the small pleasures of typesetting is the variety of material you get to read while performing your work. I hadn't read anything of a literary nature for some time, and Wynford Evans' novel promised to fill that vacuum, with possibly some unintended humour thrown in. He might even have qualified as the last man in the Twentieth Century to refer to our time as "modern".

Wynford Evans chose 10-point Optima for his novel. This was a fairly modern typeface, clean and elegant, and designed to fall between formal roman type and the spare effect of sans-serif types. Mr. Goldberg had bought the Linotype version of this type for a major contract he won in the seventies – a community college calendar. The job disappeared when the college opened its own graphics art program, complete with computer typesetting equipment. According to Arnold Cleary, Mr. Goldberg had briefly considered upgrading to keep the work, then suddenly rejected the idea in a fit of anger and sorrow.

"His face was actually red," Arnold told me. "And for the first time I heard him swear."

I asked what Mr. Goldberg had said, and Arnold smiled slightly, and said, "To hell with the bastards. To hell with them to the deepest depths of hell."

So perhaps it was appropriate that Wynford Evans chose Optima for his book. I didn't doubt that Mr. Goldberg had done some subtle persuasion as Evans flipped through our small sample book of Linotype typefaces. I was soon to find that Evans' novel was as odd as the man himself. He had typewritten the text using a fabric ribbon, which made my heart sink a little. But the first pages were clear enough, and I clipped page one onto my copy board with anticipation.

Evans had only given me twenty or so pages, and I wondered if he was still working on his great opus. I cracked my knuckles and extended my fingers over the keyboard. In my imagination my hands became birds in flight, elegant, flowing, weightless, coursing over the keys.

> As he reaches the door, Adam Rice finds the key easily enough. It is a large brass key and hangs from a spiral nail embedded in a beam near the door. A short chain hangs from the key, and at the end of the chain there is a black, iron ball, the size of a golf ball.
>
> Adam turns to look at the large room behind him. It is only half-lit, but he can see the two tables against the wall, with the shrouded figures lying motionless and flat. The third table, empty now, is against the other wall, the sheet crumpled at the foot of the table. He hadn't bothered to fold the sheet. Why would a dead man fold sheets? Why would such an unimportant thing matter? Fortunately, they had not taken off his clothes yet, though they are soiled from where he fell in the rain-washed street. Adam takes the key from its nail, and instantly the weight of the iron ball pulls his arm down to his side, and the ball strikes his shin bone. But there is no pain, and he is grateful for that. But does that mean there is no strength in his dead limbs? With both hands he lifts the key and the ball to the lock and finds that with concentration he can do this task. After some effort, he is able to insert the key into the lock, and immediately turns it a complete turn. The large metal door is counterbalanced, and swings inward with a heavy creak, a sound he remembers because it is the door they passed through when they brought him here. Adam steps into the open air, and expects to feel its freshness, expects to feel it flow into his lungs. Instead, there is nothing. A breeze does touch the skin of his face, but the sensation is

neutral. He does not breathe, nor does he need to breath. He turns and pulls the door shut, hearing the solid click of the deadbolt snap into place. Adam surveys the small, closed-in parking lot until he sees the entrance ramp.

He beings to walk towards the ramp and the streetlights burning brightly at the top of the ramp. He is glad to have a destination although he doesn't know where he will go once, he reaches the top of the ramp. He must concentrate in order to move his legs, but soon finds he can master walking without difficulty. His feet touch the concrete ramp, and he moves upward, towards the street.

CHAPTER SIX

A month after Felix Mason brought Kitty to the Queen's Inn, he decided to give her away, and specifically, to give her to me. I didn't know how long Mason had been seeing Kitty before she started coming into the shop. I know they had met in a bar downtown, one that specialized in foreign beers, and that had attracted the business crowd during the week, and the younger sophisticates on the weekend. Kitty told me this when I asked and told me even more when I pressed her for details. She was not shy about her activities, or her ambitions. As an executive assistant in a financial planning firm, she was well-placed to develop her career.

"I am smarter than most of the analysts," she told me. "And I know more about computers than they'll ever learn."

When I asked her what her plans were, she looked at me coyly.

"In time," she said simply. "You'll see, in time."

She did not tell me, however, what went wrong in her relationship with Mason, nor did I ask. Both of them were confident, selfish individuals, and it would not have taken much for one or the other to shrug off their arrangement with little hesitation, and, probably, with little emotion.

At the Queen's Inn, Mason placed a small square of paper on the table and slid it towards me. I picked it up and looked at it. There was a phone number hand-printed in the centre of the paper.

"What's this?" I said. I glanced at Sam Storry, but he was deeply into the classified section of the newspaper, the tuft of his hair visible above the edge of the paper.

"Kitty's number," Mason said. "It's yours. *She's* yours."

I looked directly at Mason. He was mildly amused, watching my reaction.

"You've been lusting after her since you first saw her," he said. "And I think she kind of likes you."

He paused to light a cigarette, then blew smoke downwards, onto the table. I slid the paper back toward him. Sam Storry was not looking up from his newspaper.

"What are you talking about?" I said carefully. I didn't know Mason well enough. He could put me off balance easily and often did it for no other reason than to amuse himself.

"She's yours," he said. "Just call her up. She won't mind."

"You don't give people away," I said.

Mason smiled, "It's done all the time." I struggled with my own reactions. In spite of the immediate anger his arrogance provoked in me, there was something else, a simpler, more urgent, and more despicable reaction – optimism.

"That's ridiculous," I said finally, looking at the square of the paper.

Mason shrugged.

"If you don't want her, I'll give her to Cowlick."

Sam closed his paper and lowered it to his knees. "I'm married," he said, though there was a frown of interest on his face. I hoped I was not so obvious.

"So was I," I said.

I wondered what Clare would think of Mason's offer. She would urge me to take it, probably. Before she left, she had seemed a little concerned about me. I could imagine her voice, the inflection of her words as if she was at the table with us, her head cocked to one side, the even white teeth glinting in the dark air.

"Why not give it a try? You never know." I reached across the table and picked up the piece of paper.

"You've just sold your soul," Mason said, grinning.

"I didn't say I'm going to call her."

Mason nodded, "yeah, sure." Then he leaned towards me, his expression serious. "She's asked about you, for Christ's sake. Just dial the number."

"Don't think you're giving her to me."

"Call it what you want."

"What happened between you two? I thought you were pretty close." Mason shook his head.

"None of your business. If you don't want her, give the number to Sam."

"I said I'm married," Sam said, looking at the square of paper in my fingers. I folded the paper and shoved it into my shirt pocket.

"So was I," I repeated.

There were times when I felt as if I lived and worked in a dead past filled with voices and echoes of voices. There were no friends in the world of Galaxy Press, only the people I worked with – the kinds of friends who disappeared when the work disappeared.

In the beginning, after the divorce, I would leave the machine and move into the outside world. But many of our friends had been mutual friends. Clare and I were a couple and had moved in a world of couples. Individuals rarely showed up at parties, or gatherings, alone. They continued to live out there, someplace, but no one cared where, or with whom. Some of the children, who had grown up together, maintained contact for a while, but inevitably even they could no longer arouse the energy into support what was, in the end, irretrievably broken. Clare and I had no children, so there wasn't even that physical reality to help maintain the group's bond. No doubt she still saw her closest friends, but if she did, I knew nothing about it.

Galaxy Press hadn't changed, but everything outside the chipped wooden door at the front of the shop had been transformed. For almost a year I went to the shop as if it were home, and to the machine as if it were my closest companion. I even began to compose meditations on the machine again, as I had done when Clare and I first met. Since I worked on a device that transmuted authorial script into lead type, I was close to the reality of writing and its production. I didn't write much on my own, however. I simply typeset fragments of ideas while producing commercial work, and in whatever typeface I happened to be using. It was a simple matter to pick up the type off the tray and set it aside for later, when I could pull a proof, and admire my output in its clear, purified form. I once imagined putting all of these pieces together into a book, and calling it *Notes from the Machine*, something like James Joyce's book of epiphanies. Though, certainly, I was no James Joyce.

Once I made the mistake of leaving one of these notes in the text of a Masonic manual, and Elizabeth Begg circled the paragraph with her greasy red pencil, drawing a huge question mark in the margin of the proof. The piece was only mildly embarrassing – a mediation on a vacant landscape – and I doubt that Elizabeth paid much attention to it, other than to show me, as clearly as she could, that it didn't belong in the text. Such typographic ruminations ended after I experimented with the importance of Clare's name to me. I set line after line of just her name until, like a child repeating a word a hundred times or more, the name lost its meaning and importance, leaving behind inly the pain. According to Professor James, the first word, the *numen prima,* was uttered by an early man (not a woman), and that the word was probably *ma, or mama.* From this the professor extrapolates the formation of entire vocabularies and the languages that contain them. His critics contemptuously call this the Jamesian ma-ma machine. For me the only useful part of his theory is that it makes no difference whether *ma* is spoken, drummed, written or printed – it is, and remains ma. In a rare, humorous aside, the professor suggests that the word accounts for man's endless fascination with the mammalian glands of women.

On the keyboard of my machine – which also begins with *ma* – the letters emerge from the middle finger of the right hand, and the index finder of the left. Extending ma to mother, all the keys of the longer word are connected to at least one of the other keys, forming an acrostic design that resembles, at best, a rocking chair. By this time other matters had begun to preoccupy me. Kitty was now a possibility in my life. Galaxy Press was becoming increasingly endangered. Adam Rice's "odyssey" was keeping me busy. And Harvey had drowned in his little quarry.

CHAPTER SEVEN

Harvey Wells' summing up should have come after his return from drowning. Instead, it occurred a week before his death and resurrection. We would argue about this afterwards, and we would use these words – death and resurrection – they seemed appropriate when talking about Harvey, though he was probably the least Christ-like individual I had ever encountered.

"The asshole thinks of himself that way," Mason said.

I smiled, "A second coming."

"An asshole."

There wasn't much work to do the week before Harvey went on vacation. He had his stone cleared of everything that wasn't current, and he had wiped its surface several times with a rag soaked with type wash.

"If it isn't like this when I come back," he told me, "There'll be shit to be raised."

The pressmen and I would share Harvey's work after he left. I had been trained as a compositor and could hand-set type from the job cases and assemble the jobs on Harvey's work bank. I could also do stonework, and what I couldn't do, the pressmen could help me with. Harvey would be missed, but we could survive without him. And just as clearly, the shop could survive without any single one of us, including me. Without Mr. Goldberg, however, it would die swiftly and permanently.

On his last Friday, Harvey came to work carrying two bags. One was his usual small shopping bag in which he carried his lunch and thermos. The other was a dark blue, nylon travel bag. He placed the nylon bag on top of one of the type cases, in plain view. At 10 o'clock, at the start of the break, he shifted the bag to his stone and began to extract its contents, placing each item carefully on the stone. Felix Mason was already at the stone, smoking and drinking coffee, and watching Harvey with mild interest. I carried my coffee to the stone and joined them. Most of what Harvey took from the bag were small plastic containers – two boxes, and a plastic tube. The last item he drew from the bag was a small class olive jar. He arranged these in a neat row in front of him.

By this time Arnold Cleary and Sam Storry had joined us, drawn by the curious display. Harvey put the nylon bag on the floor and looked at us, everyone with a cup of coffee in his hands or on the stone in front of him.

"Don't leave coffee rings on the stone," Harvey said. "Unless you want sticky shit on the bottom of your type."

"What's all this?" Mason asked, nodding at the display on the stone.

The containers appeared to be a collection of dried leaves, or some kind of organic material. One held what looked like several kernels of yellow corn.

"This is me," Harvey said, grinning foolishly. "I mean, *parts* of me."

We stared at Harvey, sipped our coffee, and gazed at the collection. "It's time I got rid of this stuff," Harvey said. "It doesn't mean anything anymore."

"What's this?" Arnold Cleary asked, pointing at the bottle closest to him. We all looked at the tiny, shrivelled object inside the bottle, something resembling a blackened piece of apple peel.

"Foreskin," Harvey said.

I backed away from the stone an inch or two. So did Sam Storry, from the corner of my eye I saw the office door open, and Mr. Goldberg began walking slowly toward the group.

"It was done when I was five," Harvey said; "My mother kept it for me."

"This is a joke, right?" Mason said.

Harvey laughed loudly. "It is kind of. It got me started, anyway." He nudged the next item, a plastic pill bottle. It contained two separate objects that looked like withered peas.

"Tonsils," Arnold Cleary said. His voice was soft, almost gentle.

"Good," Harvey said, pleased. "That's exactly right."

Mr. Goldberg had stopped between Sam Storry and me and looked down at the objects without expression. When Harvey touched the small box with the pieces of corn in it, he looked around at us. It was now obvious what the objects were.

"Teeth," I said.

Harvey nodded, "Some baby, and some adult." He grinned at us with his false teeth. "My mother kept the baby teeth," he said. "I added the others."

"What was your mother?" Mason asked. "An undertaker?"

Sam Storry snickered.

"You should have seen *her* collection," Harvey said. He touched the second to last item. "Remember I was off work 10 years ago?" he said, looking at Mr. Goldberg. Mr. Goldberg shrugged, and I wondered if he had seen all of this before.

Arnold Cleary smiled and said, "Gallbladder."

Harvey bobbed his head happily. "Yes. Want to see the scar?"

"No," Mason said.

Although we all had now shifted back from the stone slightly, no one had left. One object remained to be identified, the small olive jar, with its red lid. The jar was half-full of a dark substance that looked like mud, or soiled putty that had been scraped from old windows. I did not look too closely. Felix Mason had no such qualms. He put his eyes down to the jar, then turned it with the fingers of one hand.

"I'm afraid to ask," he said.

Harvey grinned, obviously proud of himself. "Ear wax," he said.

Mason straightened and backed away immediately. Harvey's collection suddenly seemed small, and pathetic.

"Ear wax," Mason said. "You saved your ear wax."

Harvey picked up the jar. "You know how sometimes a big piece will just fall out of your ear on its own? I was so amazed by that, I began to collect it."

"Where's the dandruff?" Mason asked.

"Dandruff?"

"Where's the nail clippings, the – crud from between your toes? The – where the hell is the stinking smegma from your *dick?*"

Harvey started to laugh.

"He-he-he-he-ha – *agh!* Shit, that's good, I never thought of that. I'll start right now, today!"

This was finally too much for the rest of us. Nausea and suppressed laughter clogged high in my chest, and when it broke from my face, spittle prayed across the stone's clean surface. Arnold Cleary walked away, shaking his head, and muttering something under his breath.

At lunch, Mason took one careful bite of his sandwich, the put it down. Harvey had almost finished his. He looked a Mason, his mouth full, and raised his eyebrows.

"What's wrong?"

"You," Mason said, and drank from his glass of draft. "Looking at your ears."

This did it for me, and I laid my half-finished bun down on its cardboard plate.

"He sounds like quite the character," Kitty said.

We were sitting on the couch in Kitty's apartment. On the kitchen table, behind us, her computer screen showed a continuously moving image of space-travel, stars flowing past like a Star Trek re-run.

"But why would he want to show us that garbage?" I persisted. Our thighs were pressed together, and the warmth of Kitty's leg seeped through our clothing and into my leg.

"Why don't you ask him?" Kitty said, arching her eyebrows at me.

"He's on holidays," I said. "Anyway, we did ask him. He just said it was time to get rid of the stuff, and for some reason wanted us to see it first. Like he was proud of it for God's sake."

"Typical."

"What do you mean, typical?"

"Everyone in that place," Kitty said. "You're all from the past. Can't you see that? He was just showing you the dinosaur bones."

It was too early in the evening for me to be irritated by anything Kitty said. I knew that in a short time we would be in her brass bed, not talking, and certainly not discussing Harvey Wells and his collection of body parts.

I had called Kitty a week after Mason gave me her phone number. I had decided not to intellectualize it. In spite of what Mason said, it seemed obvious to me that Kitty had dumped him. There was no reason I shouldn't call her. She was attractive, and I needed to do something that would help to close the door on Clare and our dead marriage. And on the sorrow that dragged my heart into my intestines.

"How did you get my number?" Kitty asked.

"I asked Felix for it," I said. "You weren't coming around the shop anymore, so I thought…"

"I'm glad you called," she said, and there was an immediate stirring between us.

We went out for a drink, and I found that Kitty was a good listener and a good talker. I told her as quickly as I could about Clare, and she told me of her need for company, though not for a relationship.

"I hate that word," she said.

"I do too," I lied.

We talked briefly about mason, but Kitty was dismissive.

"We had a thing," she said. "Past tense."

We ranged over a world of topics, easily and comfortably, as if we were old friends who had not seen one another in decades. She invited me to her apartment to continue the conversation, to keep talking, to keep the sphere of comfort and attraction alive. Her bed was fitted with a huge brass frame as its head and foot, and when we inevitably ended up in it, I amused her by humming the old Bob Dylan song, *Lay Lady Lay*. Kitty had a bright, loud laugh, and her response to my own response was gratifying, and powerful. I did not stop humming the tune for an entire week.

CHAPTER EIGHT

With Harvey gone, Elizabeth Begg had one less person to pick on, so she doubled up on her criticism of my work.

"Why did you change the spelling in the Adam Rice story?" she demanded.

She held my own proofs in front of my face accusingly. I took the long sheets and folded them loosely, then tucked them into the copy tray on the machine.

"Colour is spelled with a u," I said.

"That's not the way he spells it."

Elizabeth was more upset than necessary. She had clasped her hands together and was frowning painfully.

"I'm a better speller than Evans," I said. "Do you want him to look like an idiot?"

"I'm going to mention it to Mr. Goldberg," she said, still standing rigidly beside me, still refusing to give it up.

"What's wrong?" I asked, softening my voice a little.

Elizabeth shook her head.

"Nothing. I just wish you wouldn't change things without asking." Abruptly, she turned and walked away.

It was hard to know what was bothering her. Mr. Goldberg had not been feeling well for a couple of days, and that always upset her – she often reacted to Mr. Goldberg as if she were physically and emotionally wired into his life. Perhaps she was. Perhaps she secretly loved him and had loved him for decades. That was not so unusual for someone in her position. Or she might simply be upset by the Adam Rice story. I had seen the books Elizabeth borrowed from the downtown branch of the library, mostly historical fiction, and novels by well-known women writers. The books that sometimes lay on her desk were popular, and well-used by library customers. What must she think of a story about a dead man walking the land, looking for who-knows-what? On the other hand, she might have just hated the way I spelled colour.

"I don't know," Kitty said. "I kind of like her." I had brought her supper, a take-out order of Chinese food from a dingy restaurant not far from my own apartment. Balled chicken was my favorite dish when I didn't feel like cooking

"You *like* Elizabeth Begg?" I said, frowning.

She shrugged, collapsing a small cardboard box into the paper bag. "She's just trying to survive, you know"

I had seen Kitty occasionally talk to Elizabeth, but the secretary had always acted coldly to Kitty. Her tiny, straight body had appeared to confront Kitty's larger, sensuous form as if she were an enemy.

"She is very mother-like, don't you think?" Kitty said, raising her eyebrows at me.

At times it was difficult to know if Kitty was serious or setting a trap for me.

"She might even *be* someone's mother, I said carefully.

Kitty ignored the sarcasm.

"Just think," she said. "She has to be with you guys *every day. I* can't imagine being locked up in that gloomy shop with a pack of men dedicated to recreating the past."

"We're not recreating it," I said, foolishly taking the bait. "We're living it. It's the world we know – and it's a damn *good* world."

"It's a dead world," she said, looking directly at me. "And all of you are dead men, waiting for someone to bury you."

"Have you been reading *The Odyssey of Adam Rice?*" I asked, surprised.

She stood up. "Right now, I've got an appointment on my machine. E-mail."

"A lover, no doubt," I said flatly. "Can sperm swim through that thing?"

Kitty smiled serenely. "More than sperm. Much more."

It was about this time that I began to understand why Mason had given up on Kitty. Why had given her to me.

51

Kitty and I never got very deeply into what Professor James called the "theoretical reality of language". To begin with, neither of us were academics. In the parlance of the times, Kitty was a consumer of electronic media. I was a dinosaur. A Luddite. A revisionist. And a few other less savory things. In spite of this Kitty and I were dancers on the floor of time – another Jamesian metaphor. We danced, according to this concept, to the music in the air. It did not matter to us, or anybody, whether the sound came from a live band, a CD, a magnetic tape, or a vinyl record. According to the professor our dance remained passionate in spite of the medium. He used the sound of a single drumbeat to illustrate his point: the drumbeat, the sound of the drumbeat, was the word. Our bodies, our minds our souls, responded to the drumbeat, not to what produced it.

When I read this idea in *Verbum Sanctus,* I was excited enough to write it in the back cover of the book, determined to use it the next time Kitty – or anyone else – called me a blind, sick, dying dinosaur. Unfortunately for me, I read Professor James' work the same way people used to read Marshall McLuhan, in quick, short bites and hasty swallowings. It was a way of consuming words that had become common in the nineties and carried over into the zeros. Reading material had to be short, simple, and, if possible stupid enough to understand. So, while I mastered the easiest Jamesian *bon idée, I* did not grasp the larger context I stole it from. Kitty was intelligent enough to sense this and to demolish the idea almost as it came out of my mouth.

"How does the drumbeat reach the dancers?" she asked at lunch.

The noise clattered around us as I chewed my fish, hoping that I looked slightly cerebral, or at least reflective.

"Through the air, of course," I said carefully.

"And?"

"There is no *and.*"

Kitty smiled. "Through the air, into the ear, against the eardrum, the little bones, the what-they-are-called? Little hairs – *then* what?"

I shrugged.

"Then," she said, raising her fork, "they are converted to electronic signals that go to the appropriate section of the electronic brain." She leaned against the padded back of the seat, triumphant, or believing she was.

"You're missing the point," I said uneasily.

"Which is?"

"That the important thing, or things, are the drumbeat and the passion." Kitty shook her head. "Without the electric stuff the drumbeat would not be heard, and the passion would not be there. We could experiment."

I thought of the deaf printer I had once worked with, and how any loud noise in the shop made him jerk the same as the rest of us. He could feel the vibration in the air, he said. The louder the noise, the stronger the vibration. This did not strengthen my position, however, so I said nothing and filled my mouth with fish. Kitty's solution in any case was the best.

What he is feeling, sensing, he now realizes, is gravity. And oddly, the sense that is strongest, of all his dead faculties, is the sense of taste. He tastes gravity. It rises from the root of his tongue. This doesn't seem possible, but he reasons that the primitive earth-force is the most important force to him now. He belongs to gravity, gravity must claim in, and he wants gravity to claim him. But he is in a state of confusion. By now he should be totally with gravity, in the earth, inside the earth. There, all his senses would know gravity, just as his body mass feels its attraction in every molecule. The taste of gravity fills his mouth, passing through his tongue and flickering across the roof of the hard palate. He thinks it is metallic, then it shifts to the distinct, unpleasant taste that beer takes on when fish is being eaten. The sensation separates and congeals to intense points on the surface of the tongue, struggling to revive the taste buds. Adam decides he doesn't like the taste of gravity. Instinctively he lies flat on the ground, under a maple tree in the park, and out of sight of the street. The taste flows away from his mouth, becomes diffused in the prostrate mass of his body. Gently, he probes at his memory, curious about what is there. But his curiosity is nerveless, has no sharpness, no reason to be sharp. He lets it drift away slightly.

What does he need to know? He knows that he is here, and that there is no other fact more important. No fact except the vague concept of *'there'*. *There* is where he must be, but he does not know why, or where that place might be. The thinking is very difficult, and he stops, becoming aware once more of the ground and of his body. For now, that is enough. There is a past. But like the cells of his brain, and the tissues of his body, the past is in a state of decay. The past is decomposing. Above him the sky is obscured by the leaves of the maple tree. There is no breeze, so the leaves are very still, and form a dense pattern of blackness that is as effective as closing his eyes. The past moves closer by association. The maple leaves touch the song sometimes sung in schools, The Maple Leaf Forever… try to stay in tune, Adam, this chastisement from Mrs. Beatty, and the red-faced shame… forever the shame, forever and ever, the Sunday School, just up the street from home…

The string of associations stops, and Adam lies motionless for several minutes, waiting for the string to start again…the string hanging between your legs…that's what it is, a piece of string, and the ugly face of a girl he knows well, but whose name is completely lost in decay, in the dirt where there was a cell of memory…dirt and dirty, sex is…his mother's words, but not spoken to anyone…she lies in a building with other women, all of them old, next to her someone has soiled the bed, dirtied it… and he stepped in dog dirt while in Cuba, taking a photograph in the small park with a palm tree framing the figure…but the figure is gone, decomposed…*hay golpes en la vida*…what is that? Where does it come from? There are blows in life so strong, Cesar Vallejo, a Spanish poet in a school without a name…

In the darkness, near him, something moves, in animal of the night. After a moment, it moves away, and he sees the dim form of a raccoon, a thief in the night. The memories, he knows, are not lost. They have ceased to exist. And soon the fragments that are there will also be gone. The blows in life will no longer be blows. Nothing will have a name.

CHAPTER NINE

I had been working in the trade for 23 years, 15 of those years at Galaxy Press. After about ten years at Galaxy, I started having headaches. The headaches came on Saturdays, starting gradually in the morning and building to their greatest intensity by one or two o'clock in the afternoon. At first, I thought it was simple stress, or tension. There was a certain amount of both in the printing trade. Customers demanded work on tight deadlines, and it was always Elizabeth Begg who delivered the pressure from these customers. Often the machine acted up, usually at exactly the time Elizabeth was making her demands. The machine was also sensitive to disturbances in the atmosphere, whether it was an eruption of sunspots, surges in the city's electrical grid, ions in the atmosphere, or emotional disturbances from human beings. Felix Mason was intrigued by this idea.

"I guess you have to think like that to work on these things," he said when I tried to convince him my lines of type were honeycombed because of the temperature of a particular hot day. And, I reasoned, whatever troubled or disturbed the machine affected me directly and was no doubt partly responsible for the headaches.

Then a newspaper article about an incident in the north end of the city caught my attention. Some children from an inner school were found to be suffering common physical symptoms, including headaches and dizziness. Tests found high levels of lead deposits in the soil around the school yard. I read this story on a Saturday morning, just as my headache had begun to consolidate itself. I recalled something my grandmother had said when I first went into the printing trade as an apprentice. A big, intimidating woman, she was rooted in the end of the last century and branched out through much of the twentieth century.

"You be careful," she told me. "Printers get sick from all that lead you know. They have a sanitarium for them somewhere down in the States."

She was less interested in my health, I think, than she was about warning me of a trade she suspected was dangerous and even subversive in some way. She remembered that my grandfather, who had been a Freemason once talked about how renegade printers sometimes revealed secrets about the Masonic lodge. Only later did I discover how very possible that might be. The new knowledge that I might be poisoning myself with lead didn't worry me too much. At least it provided me with a reason for the headaches. And since they were consistent and came only on Saturdays. It was something I could live with. All workers and tradesmen had lived with the dangers of industry for the last century or so. My own father used to wash his hands in carbon-tetrachloride, which was eventually found to leach through the skin and into the substance of the body. This information came too late for my father, who died of cancer five years before retirement.

"There's none of that poisonous crap in computers," Kitty assured me. "I think you should get out of that place."

Since she told me that at least once every time we got together, I simply shrugged, and revolved my head on my neck to search for vestiges of the Saturday headache. We were at the kitchen table. As usual, the computer was on, and a complicated pattern worked itself out on the screen.

"Have you any idea how much your precious lead has poisoned the environment?"

I started to speak, but stopped, realizing I had no answer. Instead, I shrugged.

"We keep the lead to ourselves," I said. "Recycle it and use it again."

Kitty nodded with annoying complacency.

"And your headaches?"

"They're *my* headaches."

"What about the stuff you put into me?"

I laughed uneasily.

"You have a choice about that, you know."

"When you wash your hands in that disgusting sink you use, where do you think the lead particles go?"

"I'll tell you what I think," I said, wanting to get off the subject, away from the uncomfortable truth. "I think a certain amount of lead is good for you."

She laughed contemptuously. "Not for me."

"For anybody."

She shook her head and turned towards the computer.

"Is that why kids eat lead-based paint off the walls?"

It was my turn to laugh. "They don't put lead in paint anymore."

"Why not?" she said, turning to look at me, triumphant. "If it's good for you?"

"What I think," I said dully, "is that right now you need an infusion of the stuff."

She turned her chair in front of me, so that the hard ones of our knees were aligned.

"Okay," she said. "But I want it as direct as possible. "She smiled at the puzzlement on. My face. She forced my knees apart with hers and reached forward to grasp me.

"Look at that," she said. "Look at that."

"Now," she said, when she had finished, "the *prima materia* is in my guts. If I get a headache, it's your fault."

I felt I had not only lost the argument, but in some way had also been humiliated. The warm weakness I felt, lying back in the recliner chair, was the weakness of destruction. First, she had destroyed me verbally, then with the same tongue and lips had destroyed me physically. She knew this, and as she stood up and went into the bathroom, there was an unmistakable confidence in her movements. Although the headache had almost completely dissipated, I felt its roots begin to stir again, somewhere at the back and bottom of my skull, as if the lead was beginning to pool there and turn molten.

An argument to counter Kitty's victory occurred to me later, in my own apartment. Lead, I would tell her at the first opportunity, in addition to being an important substance – at the heart of the great philosophy of alchemy – was also a naturally occurring mineral in the earth. It was obvious, I would point out, that any natural substance, if it is ingested in excess, will harm you. Like tobacco smoke, or corn flakes. I thought of calling her, but knew she would just laugh, and wonder why I was still on the subject. I might also have had to defend the composition of lead that filled my machine's crucible. It was not pure lead, but an alloy that had to be hard enough for the crushing stresses of the printing press. We occasionally sent our old Linotype lines to a foundry, where it was melted, cleaned, and balanced for the proper formula. The metal came back to us in the form of long, heavy pigs, bright and gleaming, though after stacking a shipment behind the machine, my hands would get surprisingly dirty. I was glad Kitty had never seen this part of the operation. The pigs were hung individually on a hook over the crucible, and a chain automatically lowered the pig into the molten lead as the level of the lead fell. It was better than dumping used lines into the pot by hand, but some of the symbolism was lost. I could no longer see words return to their molten element, to emerge as new words, new meanings at the touch of my fingers on the keyboard. This was something I would have to explain to Kitty.

"Forget it," Felix Mason said at lunch. "You're making a big mistake."

My mistake, I realized, was to raise the subject with Mason in the first place.

"Why did you think she'd be interested in what you do?" he asked, chewing a mouthful of ham and bun.

I shook my head. "She's interested. But she wants to show us how backward we are."

"She's right about that," Mason said.

"And she *doesn't* like dirt." I added.

Mason grinned at me. "Don't you wash your hands before you do it?"

I relaxed. This is what I wanted, though I didn't have the courage to raise the subject on my own or talk about what Kitty did for me. I wanted to know if she'd done it for him, though there could be no doubt that she had.

"She didn't like the ink," Mason said, holding up one hand.

Like most printers, Mason's hands were never clean. In spite of the chemical hand cleaners, and the healing lotions we all used, ink lay in the creases of his skin, and followed the complicated patterns of pores and lines. Some pressmen, I knew, developed certain kinds of skin cancer from their work, and eventually had to quit the trade. Mason grinned and picked up the last slice of pickle from his plate. The fingers he held the pickle with looked dirty, yet wore probably cleaner than most hands in the tavern.

"She said my cock had ink on it."

"Does it?" I asked.

Mason burst into laughter, a flat, loud, unpleasant sound.

I laughed too, relieved that the topic I had raised was now broken apart, and could be abandoned.

After he had gotten control of himself, Mason asked, "have you been to see the dogs yet?"

"What dogs?"

Mason smirked. "You'll find out. She'll make sure you see the dogs."

I felt irritation that Mason could predict what might happen in my relationship with Kitty. But then I remembered, wryly, that he thought he had given her to me. As we headed back to the shop in the bright, hurtful sunlight, I found myself wondering why Mason would have ink on his cock.

CHAPTER TEN

I was finally able to surprise Kitty, to catch her off balance, as she was so fond of doing to others. She had given me one of her business cards, discreetly designed, and using the traditional Copperplate Gothic typeface. It gave her title, Executive Secretary, and her firm's name and address. Egron Incorporated was an industrial equipment supply firm, specializing in hydraulic systems. They occupied the third floor of a downtown office building, one of the older structures that had been modernized by fastening pink marble slabs to the exterior, and carpeting the narrow, dimly lit corridors. Egron's floor was large and well-lighted, however. It was laid out in cubicles, each workspace separated from its neighbours by greyish-blue fabric dividers. A wide gap between the cubicles formed a direct thoroughfare to a suite of conventional offices against the windowed wall opposite the entrance I had come through. A receptionist smiled up at me from her desk beside the door. I was not dressed for an office environment and felt a little grubby in my sports shirt and pre-pressed slacks.

"Would I be able to see Kitty Travis?" I asked.

The receptionist raised her eyebrows slightly.

"I'll check," she said. "Whom shall I say is calling?"

I gave her my name, and she picked up her telephone and spoke briefly to someone. She listened for a moment then said, "I don't know. Shall I send him in?"

She hung up and smiled at me.

"Go right in," she said, pointing down the aisle to the office area. "Through the doors."

As I walked, I caught glimpses of people at work, men in white shirts, women in conservative skirts and blouses. Telephones rang softly from invisible phones, and the air was alive with the tiny clicking sound of computer keyboards, like insects in a field. I passed through the glass doors of the office are and Kitty looked up at me from behind a large desk. The desk was L-shaped, the extension accommodating a computer and its printer. Kitty was surrounded by bookcases filled with impressive volumes with blue and red covers on top of the desk, in front of Kitty, several small piles of papers and folders were arranged in almost geometric patterns.

"What are you doing here?" she asked. She was amused and not at all upset.

"I wanted to see where you did what you do,' I said. "And to see if you wanted to go for lunch."

She glanced at her watch. "Where? The Queen's Inn?" She said this with faint distaste, and I smiled.

"Your choice," I said. "Something upscale, if you want."

"Give me a few minutes," Kitty said crisply, and I saw her as she must have been seen by others: competent, in control, important. I was impressed. This was her world, and it was far different than the world Felix Mason and I worked in. There was an aura of seriousness in Egron Incorporated, an audible hum of important business being conducted, low-pitched voices, bright fluorescent lighting, and a subtle movement of papers on desks. It was an atmosphere totally unlike the crash and clatter of Galaxy Press, which in comparison assaulted the world with mechanical power, forcing its element into the shapes we designed and urged on them. The comparison was ridiculous – Egron and the Galaxy shared almost nothing as businesses. In fact, when Egron needed to publicize itself, it would have to come to a place like Galaxy Press – or to a latter-day version of it. Kitty must have felt odd, walking out of this office and into the Galaxy.

"It's like night and day," she said, stirring her coffee. We were in a small cafeteria half a block from Egron's building and since Kitty could spare only a few minutes for lunch, we both had eaten the special: toasted tuna salad sandwich, no French fries. "Why do you think I get so worked up about the place?"

I shrugged. "You don't have anything that I would call a machine – which is what you're supposed to deal in."

"You and your machine," Kitty said, looking at me.

"Not paper orders for machines," I said, unsure where this was leading. "The machine itself. Man, and Machine." Even as I said this, I knew how pompous and silly it sounded. Yet I was absolutely serious.

Surprisingly, Kitty said, "I guess it's something I really don't understand." She glanced at her watch. "I really have to get going." She looked at me, trying to slip out of the office persona, and into the image we both knew and preferred. "Why don't you come back for a while. I'll give you a little tour of what I do."

"Next time," I said. "I have to get back to work too."

Outside the cafeteria Kitty kissed me lightly on the lips, and we parted. Fifteen minutes away the Galaxy waited for me.

When I discovered that Kitty was a practicing Catholic, I was vaguely interested. She did not have the usual icons displayed obviously in her apartment, but they were nonetheless there, place the way she lived her faith – invisibly. In the kitchen there was a small parish calendar that marked the holy days and the saint's days. There was a small, coloured illustration of Mary at the top, and the name of the church, Our Lady of Perpetual Hope. I noticed the calendar in passing, but it had no real impact on me.

Throughout my youth I had lived among Catholics, knew that my friends would date and even impregnate a Protestant woman, but rarely marry one. At one point, in adolescent despair, I considered becoming a catholic monk, and read Thomas Merton in what I considered to be dignified solitude. I learned then, and corroborated in later life, that Catholics, like everyone else, could partition their lives to a highly sophisticated degree. One of my uncles converted to the faith to marry his sweetheart. After they had two children, his wife ran off with a neighbour, leaving him a single Catholic father. Catholics were, I decided early, exactly like me.

Once I knew that Kitty was a Catholic, and presumably a confessing one, I watched for other signs. The expected crucifix was in the bedroom, hanging over the edge of the mirror on her dresser. It was actually a small rosary, made of white beads and a small white cross, all of which appeared to be made of ivory, or cream-coloured plastic. This information about Kitty's Catholicism eventually came out, as it always does. In a re-thinking period of youth, I had tried to appeal to my closest friend's reason, attempting to convince him that his religion was a farce and the pope was an arse. Until a priest warned his young parishioners not to listen to perfidious non-Catholics, who would try to undermine their faith, and my friend closed the door of his soul to my imprecations. I had no intention of asking Kitty what she confessed to her priest, or if she talked about me at all, tempting as that was. For the non-Catholic, it is both an honour and a curious kind of horror to think that a friend considers you a sinful part of their life. And the greater the sin, the deeper the horror becomes. It was better, I decided, not to know.

The theories of Catholicism were not so difficult, and were in fact, familiar ground for the curious non-adherent to any faith. Unexpectedly, the centre of Kitty's religion provided me with one of my best arguments. On a rainy Saturday morning we both struggled to find a section of the sheet that was not clammy and wet from our lovemaking.

"Eeeg! That's horrible," Kitty shrieked.

"It's probably yours," I said defensively, then recoiled from a cold, damp spot, something slick and smooth. Finally, we found enough clean space to stop moving and lay quietly in the gloom, listening to the rain on the bedroom window.

"It's good stuff," I said, unconvincingly. "The essential fluid, like holy water."

"Not from you it isn't," Kitty said.

I was hurt. "I would compare it with any priest's any day."

"Be careful," Kitty said, but there was amusement in her voice. "Next you'll be telling me it's as pure as the lead in your bloody machine." It was impossible to carry on the conversation lying down, and I sat up, throwing off the sheet. Kitty raised herself onto her elbows.

"The lead," I said, "is purer than you can imagine."

"How pure? Go on, tell me."

"You might compare it to your mass – to…" I hesitated, wanting to get it right – "transubstantiation."

Kitty laughed. "You haven't a clue what you're talking about."

"Give me some credit," I said. "The lead is not just words in symbolic form. Lead is …" I paused again. "Lead is the actual, real, true, blood of language itself."

Kitty didn't say anything, and the rain washed quietly on the window.

"What's wrong?" I asked. "Can't comprehend the miracle of it?"

"You bastard," Kitty said, and grabbed me roughly in one hand. "I'm taking you to confession."

"With my dick in your hand?"

"And your nose in the other hand."

We got up, and Kitty went into the kitchen and filled the kettle. The conversation, like most of our banter, was forgotten. Yet I felt I had made my point. And probably had committed a serious sin. Kitty's momentary silence was an indication of my success, and even hour later, I glowed with my own intellectual inflation.

CHAPTER ELEVEN

When Elizabeth Begg started to bang on the office door with a wooden ruler, I thought something was wrong with my machine. I jumped out of my chair and stood away from the mold wheel, then saw Elizabeth at the office door, whacking the ruler against the door's wooden panels. She kept up the steady, annoying racket until everyone had looked up from their work. Then she summoned us with a circular gesture of her arm. At first, no one moved, but when she repeated the movement vigorously enough to shake her whole body, the machines were stopped, and we began to move toward the office. When we were assembled in front of her, Elizabeth stepped to one side and Mr. Goldberg came forward. He looked worried.

"Harvey's had an accident," he said.

No one said anything.

"All I know is what Alice – his wife – told me," he went on. His hands rose awkwardly from his sides, then fell back against his pant legs. "He was swimming, and got into trouble, somehow. I don't know really what happened."

"Is he dead?" Felix Mason asked.

Mr. Goldberg shook his head quickly. "No, but he's in a coma, nearly dead, I guess. He almost drowned."

"Dear Lord," Arnold Cleary said. "Where is he now?"

"At the General. In pretty bad shape. If anyone wants to go – let me know."

"How long before you know something?" I asked. A curious tightness had gathered below my diaphragm.

"I don't know," Mr. Goldberg said. "I can't tell you anything more, right now. I guess we'll have to wait."

Elizabeth Begg stepped an inch forward.

"I'll be collecting for flowers," she said evenly but her voice trembled slightly. As we returned to work, we had to pass Harvey's stone, and I glanced at it curiously, trying to imagine it without Harvey Wells. It would need to be cleaned, I thought, in case he came back.

Most of us went to the Queen's Inn at moon, drawn by the tragedy that had abruptly fallen upon Galaxy Press. Mason tried to be distant, but he avoided his usual attacks on Harvey's personality. No one said much, and when I suggested we toast Harvey the response, like the toast itself, was weak and reluctant. Later in the afternoon, just before quitting time, Harvey's wife Alice came to the shop to talk to Mr. Goldberg. The office door was open, and I watched as she spoke quietly to Mr. Goldberg and Elizabeth Begg. I had met Alice a few times over the years. She was a small, slight woman, with a pale, powdery complexion. She wore clothes that matched her appearance, and she seemed to blend into whatever room or setting she occupied. Now, stricken by Harvey's accident, she looked almost transparent, though outwardly her appearance had changed very little. Both Mr. Goldberg and Elizabeth were leaning forward as Alice spoke, and I knew they were trying to catch every word the woman said, speaking in her soft, rapid monotone. For her sake, I hoped Harvey would survive.

In my apartment, I watched the news and though of calling Kitty. Then, for no reason, I wondered if Harvey ever kissed Alice's breasts, which were small but apparently well-formed. I struggled with the image, which quickly reverted to one I could imagine perfectly, and in greater detail. The only image of our marriage, the image that came to me repeatedly and often, was of the night I first kissed Claire's breasts, actually before we were married. I remembered it as a tender, sweet act, and on the basis of her reaction and her willingness to let me do it again and again, we decided to get married. And although I continued to kiss her breasts, only the first time I did this returned to haunt me, to remind me what I had lost and could never recover. When I recalled the painful years of our marriage it amazed me, we could not sustain that first simple joy, that pleasure of kissing her breasts, and of her breasts being kissed.

At the pub, Sam Storry seemed more taciturn than ever, and buried himself even more deeply into his newspaper. Although he claimed to have his new job lined up, he appeared to still be searching for something else.

"Let me know if you find anything good," Mason said to the back of the paper. "I might apply." Sam did not respond, did not appear to have heard Mason's voice.

"Are you going to the hospital?" I asked Mason. He shook his head and did not answer, and I immediately regretted asking the question.

After a moment or so, he said, "There's nothing to go for. He's out of it. Brain dead."

This time I shook my head.

"Not according to Arnold. A doctor told him they're not sure – they should know in the next couple of days."

Mason shrugged.

"Tell me when you find out. But I won't be a hypocrite."

This angered me.

"What the hell do you mean? How is going to see the man make you a hypocrite?"

He sneered.

"I don't feel any different about him. He's still an asshole."

I could not condemn him for his honesty, but I found it hard to understand. My own reaction was difficult enough for me to comprehend. When I thought of Harvey, it was as if I could not quite catch my breath, as if, like Harvey, I had been submerged in the quarry behind his house, which I visited once, five years before. Harvey had invited everyone to his place for a staff picnic. It had been a strange and strained affair that did not last into the evening. Harvey's house was on a secondary road at the edge of the city. His nearest neighbour was a quarter of a mile away. The tow-story house was old, and the yellow clapboard needed painting. Like many rural houses, there was an enormous 200-foot-deep yard behind the house, enclosed by a post-and-wire fence. A yard, and not far from the shed was a brick barbecue Harvey had built himself.

"Just call me a stonemason," Harvey had laughed. "I even have a trowel." He had gone to the tool shed to get the trowel to show us and laughed like a fool as he held it aloft. Fifty yards beyond Harvey's property was an abandoned stone quarry filled with water. Harvey used it frequently for swimming, though he had to share it with teenagers who arrived in Chevettes, and sometimes on bicycles.

"Still," he said, "it's like having my own private, natural pool." Water had collected in the quarry through a combination of rain and seepage from the water table. Harvey claimed it was spring fed, but its stale taste and smell wasn't reassuring. That afternoon Harvey had impressed everyone in his athletics. Stripped down to a pair of blue boxer shorts, he did a few calisthenics at the edge of the quarry, showing off a firm, trim physique. Then he dove from a rocky ledge into the murky water.

"Damn fool," Mr. Goldberg had said, shaking his head in amazement. Like many others, Mr. Goldberg had not changed his clothes, nor even came close to the edge of the water.

I looked at Mason in the Queen's Inn and made a decision.

"I think I'll go and see him," I said. "Maybe tomorrow."

Felix shrugged and remained silent. Nothing had changed between Felix Mason and me once I started to see Kitty regularly. He remained a difficult, arrogant individual, and although we continued to drink together, our friendship – if it could be called that – remained superficial and lacked enthusiasm. I was ashamed of the first urge I had felt to share our knowledge of Kitty, as if he had once really possessed her in some way. No doubt, in his own mind, he thought he had given away another human being. I would not allow myself to enter that very small, and personal illusion, refused to become what he wanted me to be – some sort of minor actor in the play of his life.

The shop was only two blocks from the Queen's Inn, a quick five-minute walk. This usually allowed us to extend our lunch to the last possible moment, and to make the swift, final toast to Benjamin Franklin. Since we had already toasted Harvey, we skipped the Franklin salute. On the street someone behind us called my name. I looked back at the small old man we had just passed. Felix Mason and Sam Storry turned their heads but did not slow down. With shock, I recognized the man as Danny Ellis. I stopped and waved the other two on. I had thought Danny was just another wino because he looked like one. His five-day stubble was white and greasy. His hair, which had always been neat, was swept by the breeze, and – except for its yellowish whiteness – looked like Sam Storry's thatch. His clothes were baggy and unpressed, and the sleeves of his plaid shirt were rolled untidily half-way up his forearms. We shook hands, and Danny looked at me hopefully. His pale blue eyes were soft and surrounded by puffy, lined skin. He must have been nearing seventy by this time. He reeked of cheap sherry.

"What are you doing these days?" he asked. I told him and he nodded and brushed at his hair.

"Do they need anyone?" he said. "For a few hours a week? Think maybe you could ask for me?" It was awkward. I told Danny he could use my name, but that I didn't think that there was much typesetting to be done. How could I tell him we were all paddling in a backwater of the trade that might dry up at any moment? I had worked with Danny before I went to Galaxy Press. Both of us were Linotype operators at Cooper Press, a poorly managed print shop on the other side of town. It was there that I first got to work on the machine. An operator had retired, leaving Danny Ellis and wo cranky machines, both predating the war. Danny himself was a fussy, solitary man when we first met, and he hadn't changed. The job was perfect for him. He had minimal contact with the pressmen, or the other compositors, and was happy just communicating with his machine, a rare No. 5 model. He actually talked to the Linotype, in half mumbles and occasional sentences spoken out loud. It was unnerving to be near him. Whenever I heard his voice – usually when I was bringing a box of old lines of type to place beside his machine for re-melting – I'd look at him, but then see he was talking to his assembler elevator or his mold wheel. He was supportive however, whenever I asked him questions about the machine. If he was afraid, I would someday replace him, he didn't show it. In fact, It was Danny Ellis who taught me how to join two lines so that you couldn't tell where the break was in a body of text. Although I didn't want to admit it, even then typesetting technology was undergoing change. Offset printing techniques were making it possible to create images without using the Linotype or handset type. And Cooper Printing was among the first to embrace any changes that would cut costs in the simplest way possible, by reducing wages, or getting rid of people. At that time typewriters were being linked to offset press technology. A page of text, produced on a typewriter, could replace the lead type of a Linotype machine. The first results were a poor, ugly replacement for real type, but many customers didn't know the difference between real type and imitations of type. And, Cooper Printing had discovered, they could hire typists to do the work Linotype operators had previously done. The formula was simple and attractive for the owners: typists were almost all women, and at the time could be hired to do the work for about a third of what a journeyman printer was paid. The day one of our biggest typesetting accounts went "upstirs" to be typed, Danny Ellis stood up from his machine and hitched up his pants, then brushed back his hair with one hand. It was a patterned sequence of body movements he performed every time he rose from his machine, and probably gave him some small comfort, a slight feeling of security. He had come over to my machine, where I was cleaning the metal pot.

"What do you think's going to happen?" he asked. I was much younger than Danny, and although the changes worried me, they didn't frighten me as much as they frightened Danny.

I shrugged and said, "I guess we'll have to learn to type." I shouldn't have been so off handed. Danny stood beside me and looked with me into the metal pot of my machine. I had thoroughly skimmed the surface of the lead and the molten metal reflected light like a mirror. Danny stood quietly for a moment or two, then spoke, in the same low mumble he used when he talked to his machine.

"It looks like we're finished." Danny was right, more than either of us realized. I though it merely meant Copper Printing was sacrificing quality, and that I'd better move somewhere else. A Linotype operator could always find a job. And there were machines all over the world.

Shortly afterwards I learned that Galaxy Press needed an operator and applied for the job. Danny probably tried to find another position, but he either didn't succeed, or decided to stay at Cooper Press. He was let go two years later. He didn't belong to the typographical union and didn't have skills in either hand composition or stonework. And he couldn't type. He was one of those men who were caught at the wrong time of life, unable to change and unable to fight change. There were many like him. Mr. Goldberg would have been his salvation.

"Let me know how it goes," I said, shaking his hand again, wanting to get away, to get back to what little work I had. I thought he was going to hitch up his pants, but he didn't, he simply nodded and continued to stare into my face. When I got back to my machine, ignoring Elizabeth Begg's watchful eyes, I looked into the well of the metal pot and felt a fear I'd never experienced as strongly as I did at that moment.

CHAPTER TWELVE

The hospital was both old and new. Fresh, antiqued-red brick butted against the older city-stained red brick, which had been sandblasted to make it appear new, but had only enhanced what was obviously quite old. Harvey was in the intensive care unit, very close to where the buildings merged. Inside, the terrazzo floor was continued from the old section, the join visible only by the separation of a thin bar of brass dissecting the width of the corridor. Harvey was actually in the older building, where my father had died in the seventies. This did not make me happy, and my still living feelings for my dead parent heightened my already apprehensive state of mind.

Visitors to the intensive care unit had to be cleared at a small desk in a cubicle opening onto the terrazzo hallway. I had to identify myself and explain my relationship to Harvey. The receptionist, a middle-aged woman who wore a black dress over a white cotton blouse, looked like a nun. A logbook lay open in front of her.

"It's only supposed to be relatives," she said, looking up at me.

"He doesn't have too many relatives," I said uneasily. "We're pretty close, actually."

She picked up her phone and spoke briefly to someone on the other end. She nodded at me.

"Down the corridor, first door on the right. The nurse will take you in."

There were two doors leading into the intensive care unit. The first took me into the nurses' station, which consisted of wall-to-wall visual monitors, giving continuous information on the patients. The screens, with their restless, electric waves, reminded me of Kitty's computer. An

71

oriental nurse moved very close to me, presumably to stop me from going any father. She was quite short, and very attractive.

"Before you go in," she said, "there are a couple of things you should know." She held a chart board against her breasts and looked at me seriously. "He has been taken off the ventilator and is breathing quiet well on his own."

I looked through the window behind the nurse but could not see Harvey. There were several curtained-off areas on both sides of the large, semi-dark room.

"He is still getting oxygen," the nurse went on. "But his brain functions don't look very good."

"He's got brain damage?" I asked.

The nurse's expression did not change. She was neither too warm, nor too cool. She was neutral and matched her setting perfectly. It was obvious she wasn't going to commit herself.

"It doesn't look good," she said. "But the next twenty-four hours will tell more."

"He might die?"

"Yes."

Her matter-of-factness bothered me. Did she talk this way to Alice, the woman whose breasts Harvey may have sucked over many years? "This way," she said. I followed her through the door and between the curtained partitions. All of the partitions were open to the central aisle, and I tried not to look at the immobile figures and the equipment that sustained them. Then we stood at the foot of Harvey's bed, which seemed unusually high. Harvey was propped up and he wore a clear plastic breathing mask over his nose and mouth. He was breathing deeply and noisily, occasionally snoring. At every exhalation a brief mist appeared in the mask, then disappeared. He looked very healthy. His skin was pink and warm looking I mentioned this to the nurse.

"It's because of the oxygen," the nurse said.

"But he still might die?

She frowned. "We don't know that yet. Excuse me I've got other patients."

She left, and I felt irritated. I wanted her to care more, to be a little more human. She should hug me, or Harvey, or both of us, contain the sorrow that leaked into the room and around the bed. The idea didn't seem strange – no stranger than Harvey himself, propped up and breathing into a plastic mask, looking healthier than I had ever seen him look before. I moved to the side of the bed. On the opposite side was a heart monitor and an I.V. stand, holding a bag of transparent fluid leaking slowly into Harvey's arm. I looked down at the bedside table and saw the bouquet of flowers Elizabeth had bought and the card we had all signed. Beside our card was a larger card from Harvey's wife. I picked it up and ready her tiny, neat inscription:

My dearest darling.
Until hell freezes and the moon sets in the east.

It was a private greeting only Harvey could have understood. I replaced the card and looked at his face.

"Hot damn," I said softly. "And whoop-de-shit."

He snorted once, loudly, and I began to cry. It was out of my control. It rose from my chest and rushed from my eyes. My father's ghost moved through a room somewhere upstairs. Suddenly the nurse was at my side, handing me a Kleenex. I thanked her, and moved to the foot of the bed again, wiping my face, and sniffing loudly, without embarrassment. The nurse disappeared, leaving the Kleenex box on Harvey's bed. I regained control of myself quickly, worried that my eyes were now red, and people would know that I had been crying. The same thing had bothered me when my father died. I waved to Harvey.

"See you later," I said, and left him there.

CHAPTER THIRTEEN

THE DEAD AND UNQUIET ADAM RICE

It was impossible to shake off the illusion that some great death was sneaking over the world. The film *Apocalypse Now* was re-released on video, while new illustrated editions of the original biblical book of Revelations had been appearing in bookstores since mid-decade. Professor James was featured in both *Time* and *Maclean's* in the same week. When I left the hospital, I returned to the shop to immerse myself in the underworld activities of the dead and unquiet Adam Rice.

He would laugh if he could. But from the depths of his chest only a tremble emerges, a shudder of organs and muscles that had no strength and no purpose. No breath moves out of his mouth and nostrils, not a sound, not a whisper. From the road the cemetery looks inviting. He had walked here from the end of the bus route, drawn by the dim member of its location. He used a ticket he found on the street, and a transfer to carry him as far as the bus would take him. He watched until just after noon, when not many people were going out from the city. Neither of the bus drivers took notice of him. Neither smelled him. He sat at the back of both buses. On the last bus a group of teenagers giggled and made faces at him when they though he wasn't looking. He stared at them and wondered how anyone could be so stupid and still be alive. Since they had nothing else to do, they continued to mock him openly until their stop came. As they got off the bus, they made baboon-like sounds, and threw something in his direction, a crumpled piece of silver paper, and a crust of bread, not knowing he didn't require food.

Now, at the cemetery, he looks across the slightly rising land and its cool grass, and feels as if he is drinking, satisfying some kind of thirst.

Because his mind is slow and confused, he hasn't considered this place until now. Yet he knows it may not be that simple. The cemetery is a mixed place. The older section is littered with traditional tombstones and monuments, but to his right lies an acre of land that is separated by an asphalt road. The land is flat, and the ground-level monuments are visible only by the sunlight reflecting off their surfaces, or by the arrangement of flowers scattered here and there in the green field. There is something here that neither attracts nor repels him. It might be the silence, the completion. The years of voices that speak, shout, sing and cry no more. The anger and rage that is stilled. The love cries that have stopped. He belongs here as nowhere else. Yet he does not immediately move toward the grass, sensing the completion does not yet belong to him. He cannot understand why this is so. Finally, he chooses a good moment, and crosses the busy road. He still feels fear and might allow the brutish blue truck that is rushing at him to end it, if it would end. Instead, he waits until it passes, catching a glimpse of the driver, a bored, middle-aged man, one hand on the wheel, picking his nose with a finger of the other hand. The grass is soft on the bottom of his feet, and thick with chemical sprays. The toxins rise invisibly and touch his senses, penetrating his awareness.

> For some time, he walks, and reads inscriptions on the graves. He is in the ground-level area, and the graves all bear dates within the past seven years. Then the graves stop, and the grass is clean, well-tended, still, and waiting. It is here he finds the new holes. There are three, waiting for the newly dead. Each already has a concrete box at the bottom of the hole, ready to receive the coffin. He knows he cannot belong here. The bottom of each box is visible, with only a few grains of earth on the rough surface. He had thought to lie at the bottom and cover himself lightly, so that invisible, he would rest beneath a descending coffin. Now he sees that not only is this not possible, but it is also not what he wants to do. He does not want to lie pressed under another identity. If he is to be anonymous, it must be without another's name.

He walks back to the cemetery road and passes into the older section. Soon he is among marble and dressed stone, ornate crosses and stone lambs, blind figures of granite, cherubs and small Christs, and the tragedies of past times, when children died early of common illnesses, sometimes laid out side-by-side, siblings of death. He spends two hours here until the silent voices around him have grown tiresome. The one place he should belong to entirely, offers no hope to him, no respite. This is something that could be inscribed on a stone if a stone were ever possible for him: "no requites".

CHAPTER FOURTEEN

ROOT

In today's word (a phrase I have come to despise), the word *obsolete* means anything that is older than last year, especially if it is a piece of electronic equipment that was bought with the assurance that it was as up to date as the future. We have always lived with the addiction to newness. It was only in the last century, that it became the equivalent to gambling: spend everything with the hope of winning everything. For some businesses it worked well. For the rest of us it meant junking the past in exchanged for an uncertain, unchallenged future.

Occasionally, at flea markets, you can still see eight-track tape players and vinyl records. You can find sad sets of out-of-date encyclopedias and both manual and electric typewriters. There is a surprising abundance of dial telephone sets, crystal ashtrays, television antenna rotators and cable converters. More important than these artifacts are the people who restlessly drift past the detritus of the near and not-so-near past, members of the phenomenon Professor James calls the Great Return. Old type cases are still popular at the markets and presumably people buy them to mount on their walls and fill with tiny collectables – silver and ceramic thimbles that replace the human thumbs that once grazed over the small compartments picking up type. These cases, which old-era printer know as California job cases, speak more symbolically than collectors realize. They predate the Linotype machine and arrive in the flea market's eternal past from the deeper past created by Gutenberg and his colleagues. I have my own shrine to the Great Return: the first elevator from a scrapped Linotype, mounted on a wooden base. A steel composing stick, permanently set at 21 picas, a mystical measure I learned somewhere. A type-brush, with fine brass fibers. A hardwood type-planning block to which I attached a brass plate bearing my name. A California job case, which rests, unseen, between the headboard of my bed and the wall. And the most important treasure, a stack of yellowing newsprint proofs of notes I had made on the Linotype over the years.

Although Gutenberg changed society with his invention of moveable type – and the typecase needed to hold and organize his invention, the medieval activity of printing was intimately embedded in it time, was, like carpentry and farming, something done with the hands. for almost 500 years the compositor picked up letters from type cases and assembled them in a tool – a stick – held in the other hand. Like Harvey Wells, the compositor placed his work on galleys, added space, designed space, and created space with the pieces of lead and strips of wood that were his tools.

My apprenticeship required that I learn these mechanical functions of hand and eye, required that I learn to create my space working from the top of the job, so that the type was upside down and in reverse, until eventually the brain came to understand this as a normal perspective. Lately I am beginning to believe Professor James' Grand Return is an illusory glance into a smoked mirror. James, in his *Verbum Sanctus*, does not go back beyond the short period of half a millennium, beyond Gutenberg. He stops where McLuhan began, with his idyllic oral world. James loved the word, especially its incarnation into the substance of printing on the pages of paper books. The professor's most accurate statement is ironic: Digital technology, he claims, is an Uroboros – a serpent that consumes its own tale (like McLuhan, he enjoys and produces meaningful puns). The word "digital", he notes, comes from the Latin "digitus", or finger. Yet digital technology has little, if anything to do with manual dexterity, other than the ability to push buttons with fingers. It is entirely true, James says, and at the same time entirely untrue. Voice-activated devices require no fingers, or hands; scanners and visual-recognition systems require neither voice, nor fingers. The professor, with great sarcasm, calls this "virtual irony", an illusion that tends to consume time from both ends. It was at about this point that I gave up trying to read *Verbum Sanctus*. What I could understand was that Professor James seeks to rehabilitate the fingers of the world, which, he theorizes, are directly associated with increased cerebral function, the promotion and nurturing of synaptic "events". There are signs that the deeper the professor goes into this realm, the more adherents he loses. And since he refuses to use all the forms of communication available on the computer, his audience has become increasingly limited. How many people, like me, are happy to see words in published books that are from a well-worn font of Linotype letters? And how many would be pleased to note that a few of the brass letters had broken walls, resulting in hairlines of ink between letters? In my world, this had been an unsightly typographic defect, but was now – to me, at least – a sign of perfect, molten beauty. It is unfortunate that Professor James did not find Galaxy Press in its last days. We possessed such damaged typefaces. His books, and his concept of virtual irony, were themselves ironically produced through new-era processes. On one of the end-pages of *Verbum Sanctus* is the inscription,

'Designed and typeset in NewFont by Digicomset, Inc.'

CHAPTER FIFTEEN

Ten stories below Kitty's apartment a dog barked faintly, a lonely sound that anyone from any century could identify. A dog in the street, barking at the end of the day.

"Have you noticed," I said, "that everything is ending. Sort of in sympathy with the century."

Kitty clicked her tongue against the roof of her mouth and stood up. She wore a rose-coloured nylon blouse, a good pair of grey slacks and the red pumps, she appeared to like so much, and that I claimed weakened her professed feminist stance in life. She paced across the apartment to the kitchen area and picked up a package of computer disks from the table. She held the package in one hand and folded her arms, swelling her breasts upwards. She came across the room and stood in front of me, and let her arms fall to her sides. Her breasts were directly opposite my face. I unbuttoned her blouse and kissed her nipples. In spite of their pinkness, there were dark spots I the areola, giving them a curious, earthen look, a touch of mortality I hadn't noticed before, and that now intrigued and worried me.

"How can you be so stupid?" she said softly, as she sat down beside me. "*Everything's coming to an end*," she mimicked with mild disgust. "Don't forget there's also a lot that's beginning. You need to lighten up a little," she said. "Tomorrow we'll go and see my dogs."

Kitty's dogs were kept by a girlfriend who lived on a small property outside the city. The woman did it as a sideline to her regular work downtown and had kennels for a number of dogs whose owners wanted to give them the freedom of the outdoors, or to board them for a week or so. I didn't ask how kennels could qualify as any kind of freedom. Kitty drove swiftly through the bright Saturday morning, eager to be out of the city. In the trunk of her Oldsmobile there was a wooden picnic basket she had prepared before we left. The property was small, by rural standards. Although the house was two hundred yards from the road, the land itself consisted of less than an acre. The house was a one-story dwelling, built entirely of fieldstone, and surrounded by a wooden verandah that had been recently reconstructed.

"It's a historic building," Kitty said, as we bumped over the single lane entrance. "At least Liana says it is."

The driveway went past the house toward a small, wooden barn at the rear of the property. A huge cloud of dust followed us along the driveway and sifted down on her Oldsmobile. She stopped just behind the stone house and beeped her horn once. Not far from the barn was a newer building, a long, low structure mad of cinder blocks, with a wide, shingled roof. Several barred windows ran the length of the building. As we got out of the car, a young woman emerged from the back door of the house. She was very attractive, in her late twenties, with blonde hair tied up with a red bandanna. She wore a plaid shirt and faded jeans that fit very snugly.

"Liana," Kitty said, and the two embraced.

For a moment they looked like mother and daughter. Then Kitty pulled Liana closer to me.

"This is the friend I've been telling you about," she said to Liana. "This is Liana."

We shook hands and she smiled warmly.

"Nice to meet you," she said.

I nodded. "Same here."

She was obviously too young for me, a fact that stabbed curiously at my heart.

"So, you want to take the guys out," Liana said. "They're looking forward to it."

We were midway between the barn and the kennels when Liana stopped abruptly.

"First you have to see my new wheels," she said.

She led us to the barn and went through a warped door at the side of the old building. She touched a light switch and stood aside so we could see the vehicle. It was a new DMX, fire-engine red, and studded with chrome accessories.

"My God," Kitty said, shaking her head.

Lina was obviously pleased with her toy, and I wondered what she did for a living or what her husband if.

"Okay, enough drooling," she said happily, and took us back outside.

Kitty's three dogs were overwhelmed to see her when Liana unlocked their large kennel, which opened in the rear to quite a large, fenced-in running area outside. The three animals were full-grown huskies and filled with the energy of youth. They pranced around us barking and striking us in the chest with their large paws. I was frightened, but had expected this, and was determined not to show my fear. One of the animals snapped its jaws in front of my throat and my bowels shifted queasily.

"Don't worry," Kitty said, "they're just being friendly."

She introduced me as Arturo, Renaldo, and Elena, and fearfully, I offered my hand to each of them. They in turn sniffed, snarled, and licked my fingers.

"Why Spanish names?" I asked.

Kitty shrugged and frowned, "why not?"

The dogs tumbled eagerly into the back seat of Kitty's car, and as she drove away from the house, one of the animals stuck its muzzle against my ear and breathed its hot, excited breath over the side of my face. Kitty laughed. Behind us, Liana waved one arm in the air, then dashed out of the dust storm we left behind. Kitty drove about two miles, then entered what looked like another farm road, but with no sign of a house. We stopped at the edge of a field that was almost totally enclosed on three sides by irregular lines of trees, mostly poplars and maples. The maples showed the silvery undersides of their leaves in the afternoon breeze. The field was filled with tall grass, and the breeze moved it in long waves and patterns, creating an illusion of flowing water.

It abruptly occurred to me that we were on the opposite side of the city from Harvey Wells' place, and the pool of water he nearly drowned in. Kitty let the dogs out, then removed the basket from the trunk of the car. The dogs at first were uncertain what they were going to do. For a moment it looked as if they were going to attack me and tear me to pieces, but after a few swift smells to refresh their memory, they burst away and plunged into the field. Almost immediately they split up and ran in three directions.

Kitty unrolled a bamboo mat beneath a poplar tree and emptied the picnic basket. She stripped a plastic sheet off a red ceramic bowl, revealing several gleaming, shelled eggs. She handed me a ragged piece of bread, thickly smeared with margarine, then unwrapped a wet towel from two cans of beer. I put the bread down on a paper napkin, took the cans from her and popped them open. Once everything was organized, I bit into an egg and tore off a small piece of the bread. I chewed for a few moments, then swallowed everything with a mouthful of beer.

There were moments like this in a marriage, when the perfection is too fragile to touch, or think about, without ruining it. Looking into the field, and listening to the invisible, barking dogs, I imagined that it could be Clare beside me, silent, eating content.

"Nice, isn't it?" Kitty said. I looked at her and nodded. "What do you think of Liana?"

"You two seem pretty close," I said.

Kitty smiled, "we're good friends. We go cruising together, occasionally."

"Cruising?"

She grinned at me. "I don't spend all my time in front of a computer."

"What does she do for a living?" Kitty gazed off at the field, watching for the dogs.

"She's an accountant. And a damn good one. We met at a seminar."

The dogs came together in the field. Although they were invisible, their barking converged somewhere near the south corner of the billowing grass.

"We got talking," Kitty said. "She told me about the kennels and the dogs."

"You bought them from her?"

She nodded. "Sort of. I've had them since they were puppies. Here they come."

One of the dogs came back with something in its mouth. Kitty jumped to her feet. "Yaagh!" What the hell've you got?"

"It's a mouse," I said. "A dead mouse."

The dog laid its prize at Kitty's feet and swept its tail in the air, waiting for approval. Instead, Kitty sent the dog out again. I kicked the mouse away gently with my toe, and we sat down again. We leaned our backs against the tree, and watched the grass flowing in front of us.

CHAPTER SIXTEEN

Harvey's condition improved suddenly, and according to Arnold Cleary, miraculously. Elizabeth Begg did not have to call a meeting to tell everyone of his awakening. Arnold quietly went around the shop and told each of us in turn. He appeared at the side of my machine, holding the long-handled broom he used to sweep the floor in front of the office. I stopped setting type and pushed in the clutch handle.

"Harvey's much better," Arnold said.

"Really?" I said, surprised. "When. – I mean, how do you know/"

"I saw him yesterday. I'll tell you at lunch."

At the Queen's Inn Arnold told us that he had visited Harvey the day before, Sunday. Alice Wells had been three with her husband, and Arnold had spoken to her briefly. She was very depressed, and on her way to the hospital chapel. Arnold was admitted to the intensive care unit and stood at Harvey's bedside while a nurse finished a few routine tasks. The nurse, an Oriental woman, had told Arnold, as she had told me, not to expect too much during his visit. But after about five minutes, just as Arnold was getting ready to leave, Harvey opened his eyes.

"What are you doing here?" he asked Arnold.

Arnold, apparently, kept calm. "Do you know where you are?" he asked.

Harvey blinked a few times, then said, "At the bottom, where else would I be?"

Felix Mason laughed. "You son-of-a gun," he said. "You cured him."

"Not me," Arnold said. "Not me at all."

"When's he coming back?" Sam Storry asked.

Arnold shook his head. "it's too soon to tell. He still has memory problems. But it seems he'll recover completely, with no harmful effects."

"The nurse was ready to bury him," I said.

"They just didn't know what would happen," Arnold explained. "If he'd got pneumonia, he probably would have died very quickly."

"Son-of-a-damn-bitch," Mason said, mimicking Harvey. "He probably planned it this way."

Arnold Cleary, who never drank more than one beer, raised his half-filled glass.

"I think we should toast Harvey's health, he said. "Again."

Arnold was so sincere and so obviously pleased with his good news that we quickly raised our glasses and clinked them against his.

"There's that bum you know," Sam Storry said as we filed out of the tavern. I peered into the dim room and saw Danny Ellis working his way between the tables, looking directly at me. I waved to him then followed the others outside. The good feeling about Harvey continued into the afternoon. Even my machine was in perfect operating condition. And within minutes after returning from the Queen's Inn, Elizabeth Begg brought out a docket for one of my favorite typesetting jobs. As she handed me the envelope it was plain that Elizabeth was also elated about the news. She wasn't smiling but there was an unusual grace and lightness to her movements I hadn't seen before. I opened the docket envelope and took out the copy for an auction catalogue. This was an expensive production. To be printed on glossy paper, with photographs and drawings. Since we still printed illustrations from zinc cuts mounted on wood blocks, these had to be ordered from Toronto. They weren't made locally anymore – one more example of the death of what is real, the hard image, the object that exists in the external world. But I had nothing to do with the photographs. I simply set the type, and after it had been corrected, Harvey put the type and the pictures together into pages and locked them up for the Heidelberg flat-bed press.

After I had changed the settings on the machine, and lifted the Times Roman magazine into place, I settled in front of the machine with anticipation and pleasure. I had hung a new pig of metal over the pot and clamped the first page of the copy onto the copy board in front of me. I double-checked the machine settings and made certain the vice block handles were tightened. I shifted my feet under the chair, and spread my fingers over the keyboard, in the proper starting position. I began to set type. The descriptions of the auction items had the tone and beauty of elegiac prose, and the adjectives fell from my fingers and through the keyboard with grace and ease, fingering in my mind even as the machine took the assembled words and transformed them into glimmering lines of type. Over the years I had absorbed many favorite words from this catalogue. I could almost taste them as they passed through me, the myriad and opulent syllables, the sinuous curves and cabriole legs, oval centres, coruscating flanges and flawless, beaded borders. I was engulfed in labyrinths of scrolled decorations – this word of my absolute favorite of all the words enticed from the keyboard. Decorate, decorated, decoration, and there were so many decorations in the catalogue, so many images to caress with my fingers and my mind. On these days the delirium of happiness lasts as long as the machine permits, as long as we move together to create this beauty, to be part of it, part of the Derby figurine of a maiden with a pitcher, clothed in delicate, decorated dress and petticoats, her head on an angle, a bemused, tragic expression on her porcelain features. My love for the girl lingers as I pass into landscapes magnificently executed in rich colours and stunning detail; I still long for her as I contemplate the incurving dimensions of a silver castor, then take in my fingers a Staffordshire Inkwell decorated with recumbent greyhounds. Incredibly, the machine continues, its lingering mechanics intricately lifting, plunging, revolving, locking, spurting, sliding on long, tooled rails, each piece returning to its polished, inner channel. The machine and I rise from the wooden floor and enter the dusty air of the shop. We turn gracefully, then begin to move sideways, past the thick walls and into a thin, ethereal atmosphere. We are very high, moving not just through space, but through time as well. But I do not look down, I cannot raise my eyes from the front of the machine, from the descending second elevator, and the spinning mold wheel; nor can I hear anything but the machine's clatter, its thousand tiny sounds, and even the rhythm of its larger actions, the rotating cams that I can't see, but that drives us through the stratosphere we have entered. My feet no longer touch the floor, they are held in the energy field that carries us forward, sideways, and always upward. We have entered a global trajectory, cascading through cerulean heights; the machine begins to roar in its operation, shouting incarnate vowels against the sky. I dare not think or stop the motion of my hands; any slight alteration of the reverie will end it, and our lucid fusion will tremble, clatter to its end. And as if the mere thought of that reality was a broken gear in the heart, the machine finally, inevitably, and tragically, loses its balance, misses an essential, mechanical point of equilibrium, and with a loud clash of metal, stops, and the waking dream ends. This, possibly the most wonderful reverie I had ever achieved on the machine, occurred the day after Harvey's resurrection.

CHAPTER SEVENTEEN

I tried to explain to Kitty how I felt when the reverie came, which was increasingly rare in the last day of Galaxy Press. We were eating at the kitchen table and Kitty listened patiently, though I could see her fingers stroking the edge of the computer keyboard. A multi-petalled rose expanded and contracted on the screen, drew circles, collapsed itself, was born again as a rose, and began another cycle of growth.

"It's very hard to explain," I said. "The closest I can come is to imagine I'm the Time Traveller in that film with…". The name refused to come.

"*The Time Machine,*" Kitty said. "Rod Taylor."

I nodded, angry at the empty spaces in my memory.

"It's as if I'm suspended in the air, moving through space and," I grimaced slightly embarrassed "across time."

"Sounds more like Rod Sterling," Kitty said, smiling.

"I knew you wouldn't understand," I said, pretending injury.

"You don't know anything about this," Kitty said, moving the keyboard slightly with her hand.

She must have touched a key, for the rose pattern disappeared instantly, and the contents of her hard disk appeared on the screen.

"You have no idea what it is to enter the ocean of information," she said.

"Talk about reverie." I nodded, feeling irritation at myself, for attempting to explain the unexplainable to someone outside the trade.

"You're right," I said. "I guess I don't."

"Shall I tell you what it's like?"

"You've already done that."

"Something happens," Kitty said, ignoring my response. "Something disappears between the mind and whenever it is I go or end up going."

She looked up at the screen, and sighed. "It's an intelligent orgasm. It's breathing under water, dying, and remembering everything there is to know."

Kitty paused and stared at her screen. I suddenly felt insignificant and tired. I felt like Danny Ellis, and a little like Adam Rice. And curiously, I felt as I imagined Mr. Goldberg must have felt.

"Did you ever think about what happens after death?" Kitty said earnestly. "How, if you're lucky, you will be taken on a tour of the universe, and all the secrets will be explained, how it all started, how it will all end. You'll meet God, if he's there, find your own perfect planet."

Kitty stopped and sighed again.

"That's good," I said, impressed with her vison. "Especially for a Catholic. It's different from what I was talking about, but it's not bad."

"Why is it so different?" she asked, not willing to let me go.

"I was talking about typesetting," I said.

A triumphant look came into Kitty's face. Her eyes actually widened slightly.

"I'm starting to typeset," she said.

"What do you mean?"

Kitty turned to her keyboard and typed briefly. The screen changed, became blank. The cursor pulsed at the upper left-hand corner of the screen.

"I'm starting a book," Kitty said.

"What kind of book?" I asked. Something inside me sank, without warning.

"A procedures book," she said. "For my company. Most of it will be typed on the word processing program. There'll be a lot of text, some graphs, some anecdotal material."

"Where does the typesetting come in?"

She pointed to the screen. "Everything you do on your old clunker of a machine; I'll do right here. I've started already and I'll show you in a day or two what I've got."

"Have you chosen typeface?" I asked. "Page sizes, things like that?" I could not hide the skepticism in my voice.

Kitty nodded.

"Not everything, but I've got the type – Times Roman."

I shrugged, trying to hide my reaction. She had the name of the typeface right. I had the same type on the machine. Had Mason told her what type to use? But that was only a small part of it. I was sure Kitty had neither the skill nor the training to design a book properly. Few people did.

"I'd like to see it," I lied.

She sensed my lack of enthusiasm and stood up abruptly.

"Liana's coming over," she said. "Do you want to hang around? You might be bored."

I thought of Liana in her faded jeans and plaid shirt, thought of her climbing out of her DMX, her long hair controlled by a strip of cloth.

"No," I said. "I've got some things to do. I'll call you tomorrow."

As I pulled out of the apartment entranceway, I scanned the road for Liana's car, fearful of seeing her and exchanging greetings, or waiting as her dream car swept past me. But she probably wouldn't see my dark Oldsmobile, wouldn't recognize it as a part of the world she moved through with red energy. She didn't appear however, and I drove home sullenly.

During those last months of my life was enclosed within a very small circle, marked at its perimeter by Kitty's apartment, and Galaxy Press. The circle funnelled into the smaller worlds of my machine, and the cage of Kitty's brass bed, then expanded to Harvey's house and the quarry behind it, and the kennels where Kitty kept her dogs, and the field they played in. Of all those orbiting points, only my apartment had no meaning for me. I spent as little time as possible there, and when I was there, I sought solace in my music and books. It was an older, three-story building, occupied mostly by families. Many of the tenants spoke other languages, giving the place a lively, multicultural flavour. A group of Filipino nurses lived down the hall from me, and the second floor was dense with the pleasant odour of chicken adobo, pancit, and sometimes – not so pleasantly – dried fish. The last companionship I had enjoyed there was with a divorced woman I had met in a bar. Within two months she had gathered her belongings and left, claiming to miss her husband, and giving me hope that Clare might someday change her mind and return to me.

Often, in the night, I had awakened with my brief companion beside me in the dark, knowing she was a stranger. She smelled strange, and her body was wrong in the hips and in its length. She was too long. In the first week I began to resent her usurpation of Clare's place in my life. The arrangement with Kitty was different. We did not live together. I was the stranger in her bed. She did not sleep at my place, nor did I want her to sleep there. When I fell asleep at Kitty's, I sometimes dreamed about the house that had escaped from its orbit. It might have been the warmth of Kitty's bed that produced such dreams, and the illusion when I awoke that I was at home, in bed, at night, in the past. I knew Kitty was beside me, and not Clare, but the illusion persisted, as the warmth of the bed enclosed me. Perhaps it was the mattress, or the temperature Kitty kept the apartment at, and nothing more. Perhaps any security for the unconscious mind existed only in a dark bed, at a certain temperature, and on a Springwall mattress.

"I'd like to meet your professor," Kitty said, closing *Verbum Sanctus* decisively.

"What would you say to him? I asked, looking at the deep ruby polish of her fingernails resting on the book's white dust jacket.

"I would ask him what kind of word 'orgasm' is."

"You mean the orgasm itself, or the vocalization of the orgasm?" Abruptly, Kitty and I had reached a new level in our relationship, had entered an abstract domain beyond my lead pot and beyond her electronic ocean.

"No," she said shaking her head. "I mean the orgasm itself. I mean it like his drum-beat."

I pointed at her computer. "See if you can send him and email and ask him." Kitty rose suddenly and the book fell with a soft clunk onto the carpet.

"That's a great idea," she said. "Let's try it."

She tried to get into an author's chat line but failed. She did find the electronic address of the professor's publisher and for the next half our she worked on her letter. I retrieved the book while she worked, and idly tried to find a reference to a sexual analogy or metaphor in the index. What I found startled me. The index offered a reference to "the book as whore, 175."

I quickly found the page. In true academic fashion the professor acknowledge that the idea originated in the work of William Gass, the American novelist and literary critic. Professor James noted in passing that he doubted Gass would approve of his thematic premise about the essential nature of the word, but then described on of the critic's novels as a good example of the book as harlot. According to the professor, the cover of Gass's novel, *The Tunnel* is openly, brazenly, and ludicrously enticing. A thick, lurid bar of red ink crosses the cover, like the garish, over-painted lips of a street whore. And in the centre of the red bar was a white circle, and opening, in which a shapeless red gob – a gob of blood? – trembled directly in front of the reader's face. Warming to his idea, the professor raved on about the enticing scent of the book's paper, its suppleness, erotic coolness, and typeface more entrancing than a woman's thigh. By this time, I was chuckling to myself, and Kitty turned from her computer to look at me. She was frowning deeply, a sure sign that she was having trouble with her letter. I handed her the book and indicated the passage I had just read. Within seconds she too was laughing, tears forming in the corners of her eyes.

"This is what passes for sex for this guy?"

"Don't knock it," I said, and ruffled the pages in her face, "until you try it." In spite of our merriment at the professor's characterization of Gass's novel, I knew that Gass probably had little to do with designing the book. That was almost certainly the task of a typographic designer or commercial artist. Someone who knew that words, and the volumes that contain them, are both sensory and sensual objects. They must appeal to the body's physical organs and the psyche's erotic essence.

Every typesetter learned these lessons early in his apprenticeship. When I took my training anything to do with women required the use of refined, graceful, and subtle typefaces. Anything that was driving, operated, or was in any way related to manly pursuits called for heavier, broad-shouldered, and bold typeface, producing ink that dominated the soft receptive paper of the page. All that changed, as quickly as the technology of printing changed. The feminine type persisted, but it might just as easily represent a society that no longer had a masculine ethos. And bright colours reduced heavy type to the red and blue aspirations of women, refined or not. Sex had risen to the surface of the visual world, just as Professor James pointed out. Typefaces in the last few years became as erotically mixed as the reorganization of human beings into various forms of habitation. Yet through it all – and this is where I found the professor so comforting – the word sailed in its sea of coloured inks and electronic waters. The ship named Ma-ma.

CHAPTER EIGHTEEN

Adam Rice stays away from the main thoroughfares, walking through the older streets, and frequently through alleyways behind the streets. He is careful not to look like he is up to no good. But he does not want a repetition of what happened the first time he walked in the open, in daylight, in freedom. People had begun to stare at him and move to the far side of the sidewalk as he passed them. Then he had looked at himself in a mirror inside a store window. He recoiled at what he saw: a sick whiteness, tinged with black, with a hint of green.

There was a roughness to his skin, as if it were soft, and about to slough away. He had immediately smelled himself, but found that there was no smell, that he had no power to smell, no power to operate the bellows of his lungs to draw air into his nasal cavity. If he did not breathe, or smell, how did he walk? Why did he walk? Why was he on the surface at all? Now he considers the questions as abstractions. The only reality is that he does walk, and that he is able to propel himself over the surface of a world he should be under, and not on top of.

Perhaps he should have stayed at the cemetery. If there is any purpose to his life, it is to find a place to bury himself. Yet, he thinks, there might be one more thing. There is still a need he cannot identify, there is something that he still wishes for. Surely it is not religion, or the companionship of the dead – both had been available in the cemetery.

From street corners he watches pedestrians, watches women as they walk by. But there is no movement in his body, which in any case is incapable of such movement. Why then watch them? If he needs the presence of a woman, should it no be one in the same condition as he was in? The questions are pointless.

Questions, he finds, have no answers. He has great patience. He does not grow tired as he stands near a tall, rough hedge, watching the street. Then, late in the afternoon, his eyes follow a slender figure moving along the street, a young woman. He moves away from the hedge in order to see her better.

Arnold Cleary became our link to Harvey during his short stay in the hospital. Mr. Goldberg gave Arnold time off in the afternoons to visit Harvey, and to report on his condition. But Harvey's swift recovery soon made the daily reports unnecessary.

"He's almost normal now," Arnold said, a week after Harvey's accident.

Arnold delivered this news during the morning coffee break. Even before the break, however, he had quietly spread the essential news on Harvey's condition. Behind the press he gave us the details and answered questions.

"Was he ever really that bad?" Sam Storry asked.

"You didn't see him," I said to Sam, irritated at the man's denseness. "He was breathing – but that's all."

"His vital signs were erratic," Arnold said. "And he had a full cardiac arrest the first day he was in the hospital."

"When is he coming back?" Felix Mason asked.

Arnold shook his head. "I'm not sure. Maybe next week."

"Next week!" Mason raised his eyebrows comically.

"The doctors are amazed too," Arnold said. "And the nurses. One nurse told me it was some kind of miracle."

"The Oriental nurse?" I asked.

Arnold nodded. "A beautiful young woman," he said.

Once it became clear that Harvey would soon be back among us, something relaxed, something that had disturbed the routine of Galaxy

Press, and that had brought uncertainty into the rhythmic racket of our machinery. On the Linotype I had typeset reflective fragments about Harvey as I worked, using whatever type I was working with. In the middle of a chapter on Adam Rice's wanderings I inserted a paragraph about Harvey, in the Optima typeface Wynford Evans had chosen.

Adam Rice may be dead, but Harvey Wels swims along, through quarries and rivers, refusing to drown, and refusing to die. He takes the hand of Adam, introduces him to Alice, and kisses all over her breasts.

In spite of the danger of projecting personal content into the machinery of the trade, printers were strangely attracted to the practice. Just as most people can read words on a page while they think about something else, typesetters could daydream while setting type. No doubt computer operators do the same thing. The odd thing about typesetting is how close to the surface the unconscious lies, and its willingness to intrude on what the conscious mind is doing. All of this was well-documented long before I was born into the century. The Freudian slips of the typesetter, however, had potentially large implications. Elizabeth had saved me from the blasphemous possibilities of on such slip. I had been setting a program for the dedication service of a Baptist community centre in the city. I was in a fine frame of mind, in the month before Clare left me for the dermatologist. In the service program was a prayer of invocation, and as I typeset the words, I imagined them being delivered in a lyrical Irish accent. *Sweet Jesus in Heaven may You look this day on our community and its hope for the future.* 'Sweet motherin' Jaysus,' I thought, wondering how it would be to sit through the stifling ceremony.

"What is this supposed to be?" Elizabeth demanded. I laughed and shook my head at the trick my brain had played on me, inserting the extra word Sweet and Jesus. But Elizabeth had not been amused. With her red pencil she had slashed the proof so severely, it looked as if it had been used to wrap a bloody wound. From that time on, I made sure I removed any personal fragments from the galley of type before proofing it and giving it to Elizabeth to read. And I tried to maintain tighter control over my ranging mind as my fingers swept over the keyboard. I was not always successful.

"If you want, I can teach you graphics," Kitty said.

Kitty was working on her procedures book on the computer. She had told me this when I arrived, and I settled down on the couch, prepared to wait. I had brought a paperback novel with me, and the television was on. As usual she had it tuned to CNN, and the babble of the world, as seen through American eyes, brightened the room with its sounds and images. At nine o'clock there was a forties' film I wanted to see, and I was prepared to change channels if Kitty was still occupied. I looked up at her when she spoke.

"I beg your pardon?"

"I can show you some basic graphic skills on the computer. Come here, sit beside me."

She pulled another kitchen chair next to her and patted its vinyl seat. I didn't move. I tried to show her that I was reading a book, and watching television, something Clare had often insisted was impossible to do. But I could not hide my reaction to her comment, a combination of contempt, anger, despair, and fear. The rush of emotion hit me unexpectedly, a sudden blow to the solar plexus that spread through my torso with cramping force.

Kitty stood up from the computer. "I've pissed you off," she said.

I shrugged, pretending to study the novel.

"Tell me," she insisted, coming around the end of the couch. "Is it because I dared to suggest there was something I might know about graphics that you don't?"

"How long have you been dabbling on that thing?" I said, jerking my head toward the computer.

Kitty took the book out of my hand and laid it on the floor, face down, and smiled.

"Four years."

"In high school," I said, "I took printing classes for four years. At the same time, I took design courses in art. Graphic design. After school I worked in a print shop – first as a bum-boy, then an apprentice. It took me six years to finish my apprenticeship. During that time, I also had to finish a complete set of lessons with the typographic union."

Kitty watched me closely as I said all of this. I spoke evenly, my breath coming in short, shallow waves. I could feel the heat in my face.

"I've been working for twenty-three years, steadily, at the trade. I've done every kind of composition you can imagine, designing and laying out work, choosing type, typesetting, putting jobs together, even doing the hand composition..."

"Like Harvey Wells?"

"Yes."

"And I dared to think I could teach you anything."

"Yes."

She was now touching my knee with her fingertips, and I could see that she was apologetic. But it had gotten hold of me, and I was not so easily calmed.

Several years before, I had listened to a lecture on typography by a professor of English literature, who talked about the damage early printers had done to literature. The lecture was part of an open house sponsored by the union local, and Harvey and I had gone with our wives. The professor, a sickly old man with stringy hair and soiled clothes, suggested that a printer might have dropped a form of type containing Shakespeare's work, then to make matters worse, had put the type back into the form in a haphazard manner, scrambling the immortal words of the dramatist. Several compositors in the room had stood up in protest, and the old professor appeared shocked at the reaction. At the end of the lecture the printers thrust their arms vigorously into the air. I found myself on my feet, and I pointed out, in a trembling, righteous tone, that printers have always regarded themselves as highly literate, and that no printer worth his papers would do what the professor suggested they did. Someone else shouted that even if they did, it would have been an improvement on the original. The professor did not stay long after that. I could not in truth vouch for the compositors of Shakespeare's time, but as a Linotype operator, I regarded myself as among the more educated of the trade.

Computer owners did not hold words in their hands, words that could poison the blood and become part of bones and tissue, so that it could not be given up without losing something essential, without losing a precise, solid centre of gravity. Kitty's words had stabbed me at that centre, more because she had spoken them so casually, as if they carried the weight of obvious truth and reason...

"What's wrong?"

In a prone position, I shrugged, my shoulders moving against the sheets.

"It's not because I hurt your goddam printer's feelings, is it?"

"Not exactly," I said.

Her hands were moving gently, coaxing, stroking, urging. But something was dead.

"I know what to do," she said, and moved downwards, lightly kissing my chest and abdomen.

As she took me in her mouth, I shrugged again, slightly, a movement that came from my dogy, on its own. I knew my body would respond, from a source that wasn't as flat and empty as I felt. I had a dream once, that I was lying dead on the ground, a hot dry wind blowing across my body, stirring my clothes and hair. I was a dead body, somewhat like Adam Rice, except Adam Rice was more animated that I was in the dream. He moved around. Walked, talked, thought, and spoke. In the dream, as now in Kitty's bed, I was flat on my back, and lifeless.

"There," she said. "That's better."

There was no doubt she could accomplish it. My body was a traitor. My body wasn't mine. The warmth spread I my pelvis and I moved my hips upward slightly.

"Um," Kitty murmured.

"Don't stop," I said, the death drifting away. "Don't ever stop."

I would not learn graphics from Kitty. I refused to learn, but in this I became a humble pupil without a will, and without a purpose. For many moments I merely existed, and I existed because Kitty showed me how to exist. This time she swallowed, and I died again, flat on the ground. Part of the ground, separate grains of soil.

CHAPTER NINETEEN

Galaxy Press was at the perimeter of the city's downtown area. Both Kitty and Liana worked in buildings less than a mile from the Galaxy. I occasionally had lunch with Kitty at restaurants somewhere between our two workplaces, but I saw Liana only once or twice in the area, driving her DMX. She appeared in the streets, usually late in the afternoon, once during lunch hour. Kitty and I had just met and were standing at the intersection outside Branchley China, a downtown landmark that was in danger of closing, like so many other downtown stores at the end of the century. As I kissed Kitty lightly on the lips, the blat of a car horn jarred us apart. Liana grinned up at us from her red car, idling at the stop light.

"Where are you going?" she said, raising her voice above the traffic noise.

Kitty motioned with her hand, shoving invisible food towards her mouth.

"Hop in – we'll go to Smirk's." The decision was swift, and Kitty made it by running around to the other side of the car. She opened the door and pushed the seat forward so I could climb into the tiny back seat. I glumly folded myself into the space, my knees buckling up in front of me.

Smirk's was a restored drive-in restaurant a half-mile away, accessible from the main street. Somehow it was surviving, drawing those old enough to be nostalgic about drive-ins, and those who were claiming the concept as their own, perhaps believing it expressed something essential in their young lives. The short drive to Smirk's was horrific. I was, and continue to be, comfortable only in the driver's seat. When forced to sit in the front passenger's side I keep my palm on the dashboard and try to warn the driver of impending disasters. In the back seat of any car, I am like a passenger in a plane, resigned to total death at any moment, unable to voice my fears about what might lie within a cloud bank we might be approaching, or falling through. There were no cloud banks near Liana and her DMX, but there were many obstructing vehicles, and concrete curbs I thought we would mount at any moment, turning the car over and crushing me even further into the tiny space of the back seat. Liana was aware of my discomfort. She laughed as she drove, and with the window down her hair flailed around her head and face. The acceleration of the car was fierce and almost uncontrolled – almost because Liana piloted the vehicle with indifference and joy. I almost envied her.

"Watch that car!" I yelled once, unable to stop myself.

The driver fortunately saw the red metal hurtling towards him, and braked suddenly, the front end of his car dipping deeply. It was an older model of my car, a dark Oldsmobile Cutlass. Our lunch was happy enough. Liana didn't trust us to eat in her car, so we went inside Smirk's small building and sat at one of the three tiny booths beside the windows. The greasy hamburgers and French fries were good but struck my stomach with uncertainty. As I ate, I watched Liana. She was a beautiful young woman, and I could see why Kitty liked being with her. I wondered if she felt some of the physical aura that Liana transmitted, that she seemed to direct my way with confidence and pleasure. It was sexual, and purely animal, and if it embraced both genders, as I though it must, then it could only be described as that wonderfully asexual word, charisma. I managed to command the front bucket seat for the return trip downtown, aware the whole time of Liana's slender legs disappearing under the dashboard.

I had promised myself that I would not discuss our relationship with Mason. But the promise started to disintegrate early in the second month, first at the edges, and finally in total collapse. I did not know Mason well enough to maintain the discretion and humour the situation demanded. We shared a woman, but not in love. We shared parts of her, as we shared parts of us.

"Did she try to make fun of your work?" I asked, catching both Mason and me off guard with the question.

Mason chewed without looking at me, then sipped from his glass.

"She couldn't," he said finally.

"Why not?"

I regretted having started the conversation but could not now retreat from it.

"She doesn't know anything about it," Mason said.

This was probably more true about Mason's work than it was about mine.

"That doesn't seem to stop her," I said.

Mason did not interrupt his eating, and I thought that he was reflecting on what I had said. Instead, when he had swallowed, and taken another drink of beer, he didn't look at me or say anything further.

"Well?"

"Well, what?"

"Didn't she tell you how obsolete you are?"

Now he looked at me, his grey eyes expressionless.

"You are nuts if you let her under your skin."

This at least told me something. I shrugged and drank from my own glass.

"I wonder why she does it."

"You want to know what I said to her."

"I shook my head. "I'm just curious."

"Fuck off." I looked at him sharply.

"What?"

"Tell her to fuck herself," Mason said. "It's that simple."

"Not very productive, though."

He grinned. "Maybe not. But pretty effective."

I tried to imagine Kitty's reaction but could not visualize it. It could not happen, of course, I could not react the way Mason reacted had he looked at her with that flat stare, and said those exact words? How would Kitty have responded?

"Time for you to go," she might have said. Or "You've used up your time." Or she might have responded just as frankly: "Okay, you bastard, get out."

My need to know what went on between Kitty and Mason and somehow perverse, and certainly useless to me. Mason would not allow himself to be cornered by anyone, and I felt sure that if Kitty had challenged him, as she did me, his response would have been as straightforward as what he had said. They both had very strong wills. It might have been Kitty who had given Mason up or had simply given him the boot. It was impossible that he had given her away, had given her to me.

101

CHAPTER TWENTY

From my position at the front of the shop, I didn't miss much that happened. I was out of my chair fairly often, clearing distributor stops at the back of the machine, or making adjustments. When the city inspectors came out of the office with Mr. Goldberg. I watched with interest, standing in front of the machine, and pretending to fiddle with the vice jaws. There were two of them, both young men in suits, and wearing white construction helmets, bearing the city logo. Each carried a clipboard. They talked earnestly to Mr. Goldberg, who waved his arm around to point out different parts of the shop. He did not turn my way. Then he led them to the far front corner of the shop, near Elizabeth's washroom. Across from the washroom was the door leading to the basement. Mr. Goldberg opened the door and reached inside to turn on the light switch. He led the way and the three men disappeared down the steep wooden steps. I knew just how steep and dangerous the steps were. I had carried a lot of my type down into the basement over the years.

We stored type for the larger jobs in the basement – company directories, catalogues, and school calendars – type that could be brought back up, corrected, and printed again the next year. There were fewer of these jobs now, which was fortunate – I did not find it as easy as I once did to lug pages of lead up and down those stairs. And in the last three years the flooding had started, turning the already gloomy basement into a wet dungeon that even the rats hated. Harvey said he saw a rat swimming in a foot of water once, swimming and enjoying himself. Doing the dog paddle, according to Harvey. None of us had believed him, and we had descended to the foot of the stairs to peer over the surface of the black water, which was absolutely motionless, and reflected the light bulbs on the ceiling beams like a dark mirror. We laughed at Harvey, but I knew from experience that rats visited the basement. I had seen their dried droppings around the piles of type, and more than once I saw a swift-moving shadow as I descended the stairs. But I had never seen a swimming rat.

When Mr. Goldberg emerged from the basement a few minutes later, he had to pause at the top of the stairs to catch his breath. The air whistled in his chest, and he place one hand against the washroom door to steady himself. The young men from the city looked alarmed, but when Mr. Goldberg waved away their concern, they relaxed and waited patiently for the old man to regain his strength. Mr. Goldberg led them into the office and shut the door behind them. I felt a growing dread for the owner, wondering what new hardship was upon him.

"Something about the land," Arnold Cleary said at the Queen's Inn.

It could not have been too serious, I though since Arnold sipped at his glass of beer delicately and with slow pleasure. We knew Arnold spoke to Mr. Goldberg privately, and with an intimacy no one else shared. Perhaps it was because they were contemporaries and knew things the rest of us were not old enough to know or understand.

"What about the land?" Mason prompted him.

Arnold put down his glass.

"There's a fault, or a sinkhole, somewhere nearby," he said. "That's what's been causing the flooding."

He paused, reaching into his trouser pocket, and pulled out a linen handkerchief. He carefully wiped away a ring of water on the table in front of him.

"Jesus Christ," Mason said impatiently.

"The city's worried there might be more movement. The sewers and watermains could be affected." Arnold looked at me. "The foundations of the Galaxy might even be in danger."

"I'm glad I'm leaving," Sam Storry said.

"So, what is Mr. Goldberg going to do?" I asked.

Arnold shrugged, and shook his head sadly.

"I don't know," he said. "I don't know."

"Well by the hell," Mason said loudly, "that be-dammed Harvey better get back pretty soon and get his rats to work."

Arnold looked at Mason and nodded.

"He is," he said. "He'll be back tomorrow morning.

Somewhere, probably in an old carboard box, there is an early photograph of my parents, two or three aunts and uncles, and their children, sitting at a kitchen table. The table, covered with a checkered oilcloth, is absolutely empty, and the people sitting around the table all have their hands in their laps. They are also smiling oddly, as if posing at posing. The photograph came to mind as we gathered around Harvey's stone the morning he came back to work. Harvey placed his hands flat on the stone's cool metal surface and beamed at us with the same inexplicable expression as my relatives wore in the old photograph. Mr. Goldberg patted Harvey on the shoulder-blades.

"We're all glad to see you back," he said.

"Me too," Harvey said.

I had made sure the stone was clear for Harvey's return, and the way Harvey's hand caressed its surface, I was glad that I had taken the trouble.

"Are you sure you're ready?" Arnold Cleary asked.

"Absolutely," Harvey said, grinning. "I've had a holiday, haven't I?"

Elizabeth Begg stood a little behind Mr. Goldberg, glancing frequently at the office watching for customers and listening for the telephone. Sam Storry stood at the end of the stone, shifting his weight from one foot to the other, obviously impatient at all the attention Harvey was getting.

"So, what was it like to drown?" he asked suddenly.

A look of irritation crossed Arnold Cleary's face, a rare expression for him. But Harvey answered immediately, and with a shrug.

"I didn't drown," he said. "I'm a good swimmer, I could never drown."

"Like the rat," Felix Mason said, then grinned at Harvey. "What were you doing at the bottom of the quarry?"

"That," Harvey said, "is something else. I'll tell you about that – what I found there."

Here we go, I thought. It seemed that he had emerged from the coma unaffected, unchanged.

Mr. Goldberg patted his should again. "It's just good to have you back," he said. "Don't work too hard. The others will help you out all they can."

Elizabeth had already returned to the office, and Sam Storry was backing away from the stone. Mason lit a cigarette, and I wondered if he would drop ashes onto the gleaming surface of the stone.

"Okay," Harvey said, slapping his palms on the stone and looking at me. "Where did you hide my jobs?" it was Harvey who suggested we go for lunch.

Arnold Cleary came, but Sam begged off. Mason neither agreed to come, nor declined, but came anyway.

"Do you remember much?" Arnold asked.

"You mean at the hospital?" Harvey said, raising his eyebrows.

Arnold nodded. "Any of it."

"I didn't drown," Harvey said. "I'm a good swimmer."

Did he realize he had just told us this? There might have been some damage after all.

"Whatever happened," I said, "how much do you remember – of any of it?"

"Everything in the water," Harvey said. "Even George coming out for me."

George was Harvey's brother-in-law. He and his wife were visiting when it happened, and George had dived into the water fully clothed to same Harvey's life.

"Then," Harvey said, "I sort of blacked out."

He spread his hands as if dismissing it as anything serious.

"Maybe a little stroke, or something." Mason snorted. "So, you dove to the bottom on purpose."

"Of course. I always do that."

"Like a fish," Mason said.

"Like the Submariner," Harvey grinned.

"I remember him," I said. "The comic book. He could breathe underwater."

Mason bent over and looked at the side of Harvey's face.

"I don't see any gills."

Harvey laughed loudly, startling a couple at a nearby table.

"It's what I found there," he said. "That's what's important."

Mason rolled his eyes. "I have a feeling you're going to show us – a little jar filled with something horrible."

Harvey chuckled. "You'll see soon enough, I'll show you."

"I can hardly wait," Mason said.

CHAPTER TWENTY-ONE

I was surprised to find Liana at Kitty's apartment that evening. They had met after work and had gone out for dinner and a couple of drinks. Both women were still in their office dress, though Kitty had already begun to loosen some of the more constricting clothing. She had the attraction women have when taking apart the façade of exterior appearance, revealing, I believed, their essential, unembellished beauty. This was a viewpoint Clare had rejected, insisting on smearing dark lipstick over her full, pale lips, and perming hair that was naturally and beautifully straight. Disguising herself, hiding herself from me. Liana sat in a kitchen chair and put her feet up on another chair. Her nails, I noticed, were the same colour as her car. She was dressed for full effect as an accountant. The business attire, however, did not conceal Liana's attractiveness. She wore a subdued, dark brown jacket and skirt that easily accommodated her sensuality. She wore little make-up that I could see and did not need any to highlight the fine structure of her features. On the left breast of her jacket was a large, simple brooch, a gold bird with a long, stylized neck, and thin, cocked legs. Sitting near her, I felt grubby and tired, but strangely alert.

"How was your day?" she asked.

"Fine," I said. "I didn't see your car outside."

Liana laughed. "I had to take it in for a blood test. I'm using the Chevy today."

She put her feet on the floor and stood up. Kitty came out of the hallway. She had changed to a pair of slacks, and I felt a vague disappointment. Liana moved towards the door.

"I'm off," she said cheerfully.

"Okay," Kitty said. "It was nice – let's do it more often."

I stayed on the couch as Liana went out. She paused and gave me a small wave, and my heart sank slightly, a now familiar feeling when she was around. Kitty flopped down on the couch beside me, and we kissed briefly.

"What a dish," I said.

"Keep your dirty thoughts to yourself," Kitty said. "She's off limits to you."

I grinned. "Of course. She's young enough to be my daughter."

"Even as a daughter. I'm giving you fair warning." Kitty stretched, and the sinews and muscles of her body creaked slightly.

"How was your friend's first day back?" Kitty asked, still sighing from her stretch.

"I'm not sure. He's kind of strange."

"All of us are," Kitty said. "Some more than others."

"I brought you something," I said.

She straightened with interest. "What is it?"

I lifted a wrinkled plastic bag from the couch beside me and reached inside. I held the small steel cup in front of Kitty, for her inspection.

"You said you like getting in there..." I nodded toward the computer, "sailing, swimming, whatever, and coming back with exciting things."

She arched her eyebrows. "And?"

I stood up and walked into the kitchen. Curious, Kitty followed me and watched as I placed the steel cup on the stove and turned the element to its highest setting. In its hardened state the lead in the cup did not look like much. A crust had formed on the surface when it had cooled, and the metal looked rough and dirty.

"We have to wait a couple of minutes," I said.

She was now involved in the experiment and played along dutifully. We sat down in front of the television and silently watched a demonstration coming live from Ottawa. Kitty smiled slightly while I crossed my arms confidently. I had lost too many points to Kitty, and her relentless claims of technological superiority. Her fear of lead as a poison had upset me, and I took her continuous contempt for lead type as an attack on the history of the trade itself.

Harvey Wells' collection of artifacts from his own body had given me the idea. At work I had ladled molten lead from the machine's crucible and filled the steel measuring cup I took from the tool cabinet. The best demonstration, I believed, was not abstract, or theoretical. It was something from the real world. The smell began to fill the apartment, a heavy, thick odour that itched in the nostrils. We went back to the kitchen and I pointed at the cup. The lead had melted, and the surface was gleaming like a tiny mirror, a miniature version of the lead pot of my Linotype machine. Kitty shrugged but didn't say anything. I reached in front of her and shut off the stove element.

"What's your point?" she asked.

"You don't need words for this," I said. "Or metaphors. It *is* words. That's where words come from, that's where words go."

"How do you get in there?"

I looked at her blankly.

"How do you get in there, how do you find the rest of the world in that cup?"

"You don't," I said. "You create the world with it."

"What's your point?"

I knew she was being deliberately obtuse.

"That," I said, pointing to the now cooling metal, "is real. It's hot and real and has weight and substance. From it, everything we think is produced."

"I don't want to swim in that," Kitty said.

I felt that I had proved clearly what the reality of words consisted of but I also knew that the demonstration had not impressed Kitty.

I pointed at her computer, and said, "I don't want to swim in *that*."

"Well," she said, shrugging, "what should we do?"

In the brass bed, Kitty stretched again, whining like a cat. She had actually slept for about fifteen minutes, snoring loudly until I nudged her, and forced her to turn on her side. But she came fully awake and was momentarily disoriented.

"I thought it was morning," she said.

I hadn't slept, and my body felt thick and fatigued. Kitty sat up and threw the sheet off. She looked down at me. I stood up and started to dress.

"I've got to work on my book," Kitty said. "What are you going to do?"

"Rent a movie," I said. "Drink some beer, eat some popcorn."

Kitty frowned. "Are you going to do all that here?"

I shook my head. "My apartment needs me. The dust balls miss me."

"Take your cup of lead with you," Kitty said.

CHAPTER TWENTY-TWO

I found out the hard way that Wynford Evans had started taking my raw proofs of his book home. I had given everything I typeset to Elizabeth, and within a day she read the material and returned it to me for corrections. After I had made the first corrections, I pulled another set of proofs which Elizabeth gave to Evans when he came in. At some point this system broke down. Either Elizabeth was too busy to read the first proofs, or Evans came too early and decided to take the proofs home. By giving Evens my first proofs, Elizabeth had broken the traditional circle of typesetting. The circle was a model Harvey Wells had invented to describe the process. Although I was used to working within the concept, I had not heard it described the way Harvey described it, shortly after I arrived at Galaxy Press. Harvey and I had been grumbling about a customer who made too many revisions on his final proofs.

"He broke the circle," Harvey said bitterly. "you can't do that. You should rot in the bottom floor of hell for doing that."

"What circle?" I asked, mildly interested.

"Our circle," Harvey said, and he immediately made a huge circle in the air with his arms.

"It's unique," he went on. "It has a beginning and end – like the Bible. But it's also a cycle, like the Buddha."

"Buddhism?"

"The Buddha. Anyway, you know how it starts. When you get the customer's copy on your machine – that's the beginning. Sort of like twelve o'clock on a clock." I was a bit uncertain about Harvey's point, but I nodded, not wanting to interrupt.

"You set the type, then pull your proofs. You give the proofs to the proof-reader – around here that's Elizabeth. She's at the quarter-past point of the circle. Follow this?"

I nodded.

"She reads the stuff and gives it back to you. You correct your mistakes and put the corrections in the type. You pull another proof which goes to the customer. Now we're halfway around the circle." He held one hand in the air the other down near his crotch. "The customer brings the proofs back, with any changes he's found, or made – the revised proofs. Okay? We are at the three-quarter mark. You correct the type again, then give it to me. I make it up into pages, or whatever, pull another set of proofs for the customer. When they come back – with one or two corrections – the circle if finished. Then it's printed. Am I right?"

He was, of course, right, and I smiled to think I had been working in circles for some years and had been unaware of it. Now, clearly, Elizabeth had eliminated the quarter-past position and jumped directly to the half-past position, making the circle into a straight line, and duplicating what had happened to the entire industry as technology speeded up typesetting. The direct result was a great increase of errors in all printed and published work. The errors were sometimes personal and unique, especially in a straight matter such as Wynford Evans' book. The mind strayed, the fingers drifted, the inevitable happened What slipped out should never have reached Wynford Evans; but the circle had been altered, flattened.

Mr. Goldberg and Wynford Evans unexpectedly appeared beside me. Without speaking Mr. Goldberg handed me a galley proof of the Adam Rice story. Evans used a different colour marking pencil than Elizabeth Begg. He used a heavy, black marker that almost obscured the type on the page. What Mr. Goldberg now pointed to with a rigid finger was clear enough, however. I cringed as I read the words enclosed in a heavily drawn black box.

> Adam Rice may be dead, but Harvey Wells swims along, through quarries and rivers, refusing to drown and refusing to die. He takes the hand of Adam, introduces him to Alice, and kisses all her breasts.

"I didn't know you were like that," Mr. Goldberg said quietly.

I looked at him and was shocked by the sorrow in his expression. His features, already sagging with his years, appeared to hang loosely on his skull. His skin was yellowish and unhealthy looking. None of what I saw in Mr. Goldberg's face was because of my stupidity in forgetting to remove the fragment from the Adam Rice story. That was merely something for Mr. Goldberg's present pain to fix upon, to momentarily ground itself in.

"What does it mean?" Wynford Evans said, his voice even and hard.

I looked up at the two men, then stood up to face them more equally. "I'm sorry," I said, spreading my hands helplessly. "It was a mistake. I was upset about Harvey –" I nodded toward Harvey, who was working on his bank. "I don't know what else to say."

Mr. Goldberg put his hand on my elbow and squeezed it.

"We had a near-tragedy," he said to Evans. "I'll explain it to you."

"Well," Evans said, then picked at his beard with a forefinger. "Make sure it's corrected – taken out, I mean."

"I'll do that right now," I said, and walked to the flat table beside the tool cabinet.

All of the type for the Adam Rice story lay in gleaming columns on the table, the printing surface darkened from having been inked for the proof press. I quickly ran my fingers down a column, then plucked out the offending lines. I held them in front of Evans and Mr. Goldberg, then put my hand over the metal pot on my machine. I lowered the lines to the surface of the metal and let them go. They disappeared into the molten metal with a slight plop.

Evans nodded shortly. "Good." Then he held out an envelope.

"More copy," Mr. Goldberg said. Some relief had entered his face, but beneath it the sorrow and age remained. Without saying anything further, he led Wynford Evans back to the office.

I sat down and removed the new copy from the envelope. I wondered why Evans didn't bring all the copy in at once. But he was an odd duck and probably had been writing the story the same way he delivered it – piece by piece. In spite of my embarrassment, I was happy to have more work for the machine, especially straight matter. There wasn't much else. Four small jobs waited to be typeset – two business cards, a stag ticket, and a Catholic commemorative card. An hour's work at best. Elizabeth had said that a special events calendar was coming, as soon as she could get the docket ready. I changed the machine settings and sank into the peregrinations of Adam Rice. I thought of starting with a paragraph about Adam and Harvey swimming together, with a rat. I giggled and drove the thought from my mind.

Adam Rice sits in the shade of a large Catalpa tree in the park, one of the few fine old trees left standing here. He has the iron and wood seat to himself. From this position he can see the traffic moving along the street at a safe distance. A little in front of him is a pedestrian walk made of interlocking bricks. Lunch time is almost over, and it is mostly shoppers and other city dwellers who pass by him now. One man, a wino, pauses to sit beside him. The man at first is reluctant to bring out his bottle, but after studying Adam for some moments, he overcomes his reticence. It is the cheapest kind of wine, and Adam wonders what it would feel like washing down his throat. But the man does not offer Adam a drink. After a few moments the wino begins to shift away from Adam, although he is already at the far end of the bench.

"See you, pal," the man says abruptly, and gets up and walks away.

Now a group of sparrows gathers at Adam's feet, waiting for something, crumbs, or a handful of seeds. He wants to give them something but has nothing except his own flesh. This might interest crows, or seagulls, but the sparrows merely act disappointed, and fly off after a few moments. It has come to this, then. To find a way of disposing of the flesh, of allowing the flesh to be consumed by the earth.

Adam does not remember having this kind of interest in nature; but now it is a necessity. The woman he had watched had reacted negatively, glancing over her shoulder, and quickening her pace. This is not a choice, he realizes. That is not away for him.

Now he thinks about those who know him although there are not many. He might telephone someone, but he finds that there is nothing in his pockets. Everything has been taken from him. Everything. And when he realizes that there are no telephone numbers in his head, he sinks back against the wood slats of the bench in resignation.

There must be something, he thinks. There must be something. An insect buzzes beside his ear, and he becomes alert. Was he sleeping? Can he sleep? Then he is aware that a man is sitting beside him.

Unlike the wino, this man, who appears almost to be a reflection of Adam, dos does not move away from him. The man is, in fact, pressed against him. This new person has a greasy beard, and the skin of his face is dirty. His eyes twitch as he stares at Adam. The man smiles, and his teeth are green.

"I know a place," he says. "We can even stretch out, you know?"

It is Adam's turn to move away. He stands up and walks some distance from the man, who has both hands in his trousers pockets. The image of embracing horror makes Adam swoon in the hot afternoon, and he knows that this is one more thing he does not seek.

CHAPTER TWENTY-THREE

Harvey was bemused at the impending physical collapse of Galaxy Press.

"Things like this happen at the end of centuries," he said, as he tightened the last quoin in a form.

"And dead men come back to life," Felix Mason said.

Mason stood at one side of the stone, smoking, waiting for Harvey to finish locking up the lob. Harvey's work area curved away behind him, in the new configuration he wanted. At the end of the curve the tombstone was propped up on a chair, as if on display. The biggest change in Harvey since his return appeared to be a softening of his usual electric behaviour. He considered situations more carefully before reacting to them and one way he managed this was to repeat what someone said, as a child repeats new words.

"You think I died, don't you?" Harvey asked, looking at Mason.

As he spoke, he lifted the corner of the form and put the end of the quoin key under it. With his fingertips he pushed at the locked-up type, probing for weak spots, for letters that might work up, or fall out on the press. Everything was tight.

"You know you did," Mason said.

I knew Mason was baiting Harvey, probing for a reaction.

"Dead men don't talk," Harvey said.

"Or give up their secrets," I said. Then added, "you didn't see any light at the end of a tunnel – or anything like that? Or forget phone numbers?"

"Just the rock," Harvey said, and stood back from the stone.

Mason lifted the form and let it fall to the end of his arm.

"When do we see this rock?" he asked.

Harvey didn't answer. Instead, he turned to his work bank and lifted a paper bag from beside the sloped surface. He put his hand into the bag and brought something out. I shifted my feet an inch or two backwards s I thought of his last display of personal artifacts. He carried the object to the make-up stone, and with a flourish placed it in the middle of the stone. It was a rock. An irregular, rough-edged rock, probably granite, and about the size of a grapefruit. Its edges and crevices were lined with a fine and pale brown dirt. Mason lifted the form back onto the stone and rested his forearm on its upended edge.

"A rock," he said.

"That's what you found at the bottom of the quarry," I said.

Harvey beamed at us. "Not just any rock. And no moon rock, either."

Sam Storry walked behind Mason, then paused, attracted to the momentary inactivity around the stone. He shuffled closer and stood beside Mason. He looked at the rock and frowned.

"I've always been looking for it," Harvey said. "Ever since the quarry filled up and the workers left."

"The rock?" I asked.

Harvey nodded. "But I didn't know what I was looking for. I just knew there was something there for me."

"How do you know this is it?" Mason asked. I was beginning to know when Mason was being sarcastic. Unlike most people, he did not inflect his words, did not exaggerate in any way the importance of a word, or a phrase. His delivery was perfect and could be mistaken for real interest.

"Good question," Harvey said. "I swam every day. It was great. It's spring-fed, you know, and in July the water's very clear. Clear as crystal, almost. Like swimming in a fishbowl."

He rested his hands on the stone, open palms toward the rock, and looked around at us, pleased that he held our attention.

"I'm a good swimmer, always have been Twenty times around the quarry every day. Every day. Well, that day I felt like I could go on forever. It was like having sex, and you never want to stop, and you don't ever seem to finish – know what I mean?"

No one responded. It was difficult enough imagining Harvey as a marathon swimmer, and almost impossible to see him struggling over his faded, passive Alice.

"Anyway, I was going around and around so much I think I started a current going. Like a whirlpool, but very slow. It might have been my imagination, I'm not sure. The current carried me to the centre of the water, then I decided to dive. It was like you said…" Harvey looked at me, "the Submariner. I could breathe underwater."

"I dreamt that once," Sam Storry said.

Mason nudged him into silence.

"I was going down," Harvey went on, "in kind of circles, like water goes down a drain. Have you seen that? I sued to watch it when I was a kid, after my mother pulled out the bathtub plug. All the bubbles and dirt swirling down the hole."

"Was there a hole?" Mason asked.

"A hole in the water, I think," Harvey said, his eyes resting on the rock. "It felt like that. It felt like I was being sucked down into a hole. Exactly like that. I've dived down there a lot, it's not that dep, maybe twelve or fifteen feet. But I went deeper this time. I kept going down. I wasn't swimming anymore, just turning and going down, like in a crazy elevator. I knew I had to reach bottom sometime, but after a while, I didn't care. I began to enjoy it. It wasn't even dark, everything was clear blue-green, and beautiful. Then I reached the bottom. It should have been all rock – I've seen it before. But this time it was sandy, with ribs like you see in the lake, ribs of sand. I was upside down when I touched bottom. My hands came flat against the sand. I could feel the little ridges on my palms. Then I saw the rock. It was about eight feet away, sitting on the sand, all by itself. There were no other rocks anywhere in sight. I started to move toward it, I don't know why. I was attracted to it, like a magnet. I was still upside down, and the waterhole was still trying to spin me around. But I moved forward on my hands. I pushed my fingers into the ridges and pulled myself toward the rock. The waterhole was following me. I finally get to the rock. It looks bigger because the water magnifies it. I reach out for it, but nothing happens. My arm doesn't move. I try the other arm – same thing, it won't move. The waterhole is sucking at me, like it is pulling me up now. I had to get the rock, though. I knew it was important. So I focus everything on the rock, and I think my arms into moving. This time I move, and I just float easily to the rock and pick it up. Once I get it in my hands, I feel very light. I begin to go up, turning around again, but in the opposite direction. Sometime around then I felt George grab my ankle. He thought I was drowning. When I told him all this, he still said he thought

I was drowning. But that's George. He wants me to think I owe him my life. He didn't see the rock in my hand until after we got to shore."

Harvey looked at Mason, then at me. He had never spoken so long without being interrupted and when he stopped, we were still listening. Mason broke the awkward moment with a chuckle.

"If I were George," Mason said, "I would have thrown you back in."

Harvey looked at Mason but did not respond. Sam Storry was already walking back to his press.

"What are you going to do with the rock?" I asked.

"I'm going to mount it somehow," Harvey said, touching the rock with his fingers.

Mason jerked the form of the make-up stone and turned away, muttering under his breath. I began to feel the need to move. Harvey was in an almost trance-like state of happiness, his fingers still caressing his rock. I turned away from the stone and walked back to my machine, awed and envious that Harvey should have experienced something so important. I sat down at my machine and rested my fingers on the keys. The usual sensation of connectedness did not happen.

CHAPTER TWENTY-FOUR

"A rock," Kitty said.

"The centre of his world right now," I said. "It's pathetic."

Kitty stood up and walked to her computer. "I don't know about that," she said. "At least he's got something."

"A rock, and Alice, his wife."

Kitty smiled. "Some people have less."

"I guess I know that" I said.

"You have your machine," she said soothingly. "It's real enough for the moment."

It was not like Kitty to be conciliatory, especially about my machine.

"There is something that holds you and me together," she added. When I didn't respond, she said, "Electricity. Both your machine and mine need electricity to work."

I shook my head. "As long as the drive wheel can be made to turn — even by a steam engine — my machine will work."

"What about the lead pot? You need electricity for that." Obviously, Kitty had been impressed by the stove demonstration.

"A lot of machines used gas jets to heat the pot," I said confidently. "What it comes down to is the skill of the craft. What Gutenberg started out with five hundred years ago."

"And where did his skill come from?"

"He learned it, taught himself."

Kitty smiled slyly. "It came from his brain. And how does his brain work?"

I realized too late where she was headed.

"Electricity," we chimed, in unison. Unexpectedly, an idea occurred to me.

"There is a serious flaw in your argument," I said.

Kitty leaned froward. "What flaw?"

I hesitated, hoping it would come out the way I intended. Kitty waited, one of her eyebrows arched slightly. And in that tiny movement she managed to convey all of her skepticism, and her confidence in her victory.

"You're right about electricity," I said carefully. "That is how our brains function."

She nodded and smiled. "Thank you."

"Hold on," I said. "There's more. All that electrical activity is still converted to mechanical processes – the vocal cords when you speak, the muscles, tendons, and fingers when you write or type. Purely mechanical movements. Not to mention the length of time all those electrical signals take to be directed and focused..."

Kitty pursed her lips and frowned doubtfully.

"In any case," I said quickly, "the mechanical limitations are there – would you agree with that?"

"Only a little," Kitty said.

Before she could go on, I continued my argument, which was now coming together for me. "These limitations – at least for me – are almost perfectly matched by the machine's limitations. You can only go as fast as the machine can go, and if you go too fast, the magazine runs out of letters, or the molds overheat."

Already Kitty was shaking her head. I raised my hand in the air to keep her in check. "The end result is that you must work at a steady, but fairly fast pace. And this seems to correspond to the brain's pace – a brain that is functioning carefully, and accurately."

"Your brain," Kitty said.

I shrugged. "I'm as good – probably better – than any operator I've known."

"But not better than me, on the computer."

"The question is," I said, struggling now, "how fast do you want to go? Do you want to control the machine, or the machine to control you?"

"If the world had to wait for your clunky machine, where would we be?"

"Better off," I said shortly.

"What did they do before the machine was invented?"

I tried to conceal my sense of defeat as I answered, "The set type by hand."

"And no doubt these hand setters..."

"Compositors," I corrected.

"...these compositors – argued that their hand work was done at a more natural pace than the machine." She moved in swiftly now, for the kill. "And before the compositors the medieval scribes could say the same thing, probably arguing that their penmanship perfectly matched the mind of God, since all they did was copy Bibles."

I attempted a sneer. "And you would say computers match the mind of God better?"

Kitty grinned. "No. they match it best."

"God is a computer," I said with mock enlightenment.

Kitty twisted one corner of her mouth upward, in a wry grimace.

"I think you're finally getting the picture."

I had one shot left, and like a beaten schoolboy, decided to use it.

"There is something on the Linotype keyboard that your QWERTY-board doesn't have."

She sighed but said nothing.

"On the first row of the keyboard, I said, "there is a hidden word." I waited but Kitty simply stared at me, her head cocked slightly.

"The word Tao," I said. "ETAOIN. Where's the 'god' in your keyboard?

Kitty didn't bother to look at her keyboard and I knew that my I've-got-something-you-don't argument had failed. It had failed with the same completeness it would have failed in the school yard, where girls would merely have giggled at the boy who so foolishly put his manhood on the line.

In my apartment I went directly to my Coronomatic electric typewriter and pulled off the plastic dust cover. I studied the small, cramped keys and was relieved to find only *as, ax,* and *ok.* I hoped that Kitty would do the same with her computer keyboard and would concede at least this small point to me. Yet I had to admit that she had mentioned something that occasionally troubled me. When Ottmar Mergenthaler introduced the first Linotype in 1886, the machine had created a minor revolution in the trade. It could produce type several times faster than hand compositors, and there must have been great fear among the printers of the period that they would be replaced by the machine. A fear I understood all too well. A little research revealed that such fear did not last long. The machine became part of the printer's trade. It still used letter press technology and most operators come from the ranks of hand compositors. That was not true of computers, which allowed individuals totally untrained in graphic arts to produce material that was ready for the press. In the beginning it did not matter that much of this material was amateurish and typographically crude. Production was what mattered. Production, efficiency, and the ability to create products with the fewest human beings possible. Kitty and I were both wrong. God was neither a computer nor a Taoist presence in a noisy machine. He was something that had not yet been discovered, and as far as I could tell, He was nowhere close to our part of the galaxy.

Kitty may not have been as happy with her victory as I thought. The next time we met told me she had a new experiment for us to try. When I reacted without enthusiasm, she punched my shoulder.

"Come on," she said. "This isn't serious stuff."

We were on the couch, and she reached behind her and touched the base of a metal lamp on the small end table. The lamp came on instantly. She removed her hand, then touched the lamp again, causing it to glow more brightly.

Kitty looked at me. "How does it do that?"

I shrugged. "Simple electronic diodes. Something like that. I've got one too."

"All right," she said. "Watch."

She touched the lamp until it turned off. She touched it again but kept her fingers on the brass base. She held her other hand over my knees.

"Touch my hand."

I touched her outstretched fingers, and the lamp grew brighter.

"Well?" I said.

"Again."

We repeated the experiment a number of times, reversing our positions, and touching different parts of each other's body – knee, foot, head, nose, elbow. I was mildly interested but couldn't explain how it worked.

"What do you think would happen if we did the same thing with the computer?"

I looked over at the blue sea of the computer's screen. "I've had enough," I said. "You're not going to tell me it will turn off?"

"That's not what I want."

I looked at her, slightly amused. With all our touching I had become aroused.

Kitty shifted closer to me. "What if I held my hand on the keyboard while you cam inside me?"

"Sounds awkward," I said.

She touched me, lightly.

"Do you think I might become electronically impregnated?"

My attention was now on the movement of her fingers

"What do you think it would look like?" she prompted.

"One eye, blue, with qwerty teeth."

She kissed me. "Not bad. Gender?"

"What do you prefer?"

"Omnisexual. Or androgenous."

It was difficult. We were balanced on the edge of the kitchen table, and kitty leaned her weight dangerously backward, causing the table to shift slightly on the floor. In this position she achieved orgasm, but I was so worried about falling, I was unable to finish. We collapsed to the floor, laughing idiotically. After she turned off the computer, we watched television, comfortably lounging at opposite ends of the couch. Our timing had become familiar, and I would soon leave, without having to explain why. If either of our moods had been different, I might have stayed.

"Do you feel anything yet?" I asked.

"A little tiny glow, way down."

A thought occurred to me and I laughed shortly.

"What?" she said.

"Someone I know who's into computers, I can't imagine him doing that – what we did."

"He wouldn't fuck the computer?"

I put my hand on her leg and got ready to rise.

"I wouldn't have thought I would."

At the door, she kissed me warmly on the lips. At home, I touched my own automatic lamp, a small cheap thing I had bought at Zellers. How many people could you add to the human chain to make it work? Then the possibility of an orgy: twenty people and a single touch lamp. But where would you find an orgy now, and who could you trust? The answer was simple. Reduce the participants to one person and a touch-lamp, a condition almost anyone could achieve, at any time. I had nothing to come back with that could match Kitty's experiment, other than to describe my machine in the instant of casting a line of type.

"it's not a competition, for God's sake," Kitty said.

She was right, of course, and I cursed myself for having made it one. The idea of competing with Kitty brought an edge to the space between us that hadn't been there before. But we both knew this was inevitable.

"Three months," she had said, the second or third time we made love. "That's the average length of an affair."

The number three was interesting. The third year, after two decades, the length of time Clare and I had been married.

"How are you feeling?" I asked.

"About what?"

"The one-eyed zygote."

Kitty grinned. "I don't feel anything," she said. "Actually, I feel completely, totally, empty. A disappointment."

I hoped that meant that we wouldn't have to try the experiment again. If she wanted sex with her computer, she would have to do it alone.

CHAPTER TWENTY-FIVE

The basement of Galaxy Press flooded suddenly, confirming the city engineers' predictions. We rarely went down there anymore and the only way we knew it had happened was by the dank odour that filled the shop when we came to work in the morning. It was a grave-like smell, heavy with the mustiness of soil and something else – a faint, pungent smell of manure, or offal – a small that was difficult to identify. The air of the shop itself recked and brought me almost to the point of gagging. Arnold Cleary immediately checked both toilets, flushing them two or three times, but emerged shaking his head. He sniffed around the sink and ran the water, and again shook his head. We all looked in the corners of the shop, carefully, in case a rat, or some other creature, lay rotting behind a cabinet, or under a machine. Again, we found nothing. Then Harvey, at his stone, stuck his arm up in the air, like a student asking permission to leave the room.

"I know that smell," he said.

He walked directly to the basement door and opened it. "Agh," he said. "Here it is."

We gathered around, as we had done before, and looked down at the black water. The last flood had not smelled like this one. And it had not been this deep – the water covered the bottom three steps.

"Do you see your rat?" Mason asked.

Mr. Goldberg had joined us and now stared at the water with the rest of us, intrigued and repelled.

"Oh my Lord," he said.

He backed away from our circle of bodies.

"I'll call the city."

Abruptly, Harvey pushed me aside and descended the stairs.

"It's got the type," he said, his voice booming up to us.

Whatever type was still stored downstairs had been piled on wooden pallets, several inches high. But not high enough. I recoiled at the thought of having to touch the soiled metal.

"Going for a swim?" Mason chuckled.

Harvey came back up the stairs.

"Something better," he said.

During the last flood Mr. Goldberg had sent Arnold out to buy a pair of knee-high rubber boots so he could wade to the drain in the middle of the basement floor to make certain it was clear. Arnold had found a piece of cardboard blocking the pipe and the water drained away as soon as he removed it. Harvey went to the cupboard at the rear of the shop and come back wearing the boots and walking like a sailor – proud, determined, and arrogant. Not the same man who had climbed out a window to escape flying birds. He pushed past us and clumped down the stairs. He splashed into the water which came dangerously close to the top of the boots. After pausing at the bottom of the stairs for a moment he moved out of sight.

"Brave little bugger," Mason said.

I descended the stairs far enough to see Harvey moving through the water. The water was very still, and as Harvey moved, small waves spread out from his legs and disappeared into the dark corners of the basement. Harvey found the drain with his foot and kicked vigorously at something. He wore a short-sleeved shirt but rolled the material up over the should of his right arm. Then he plunged his arm into the water. He straightened an enormous dead rat handing by its tail from his hand. The rat had nothing to do with the flood the engineers said. It had just blocked the drain and prevented the water from going down. The flood, they said indicated that the land-shift was worsening. They were unable to prevent what was happening because they didn't know exactly where the fault was or in which direction it would move. The water was a symptom nothing more. But if the fault came anywhere near the foundations of Galaxy Press, the consequences could be very serious.

Kitty appeared in the shop later in the afternoon. I had no idea she was coming, and I was startled to see her standing beside Felix Mason's press. I was in the act of feeding several brass letters into the machine's distributing mechanism as Kitty leaned forward to kiss Mason lightly on the lips. My face instantly heated up and I looked around the shop to see if anyone had noticed my reaction. No one was watching me. Harvey was staring openly at Kitty. Arnold looked once at her from the cutting machine then turned back to his work. Sam Storry was operating the offset press and hadn't see Kitty yet. No one was aware of my shock and the sick fear that rose into my chest.

Kitty wore a dark, knitted dress that clung closely to her body. A silver belt drew the material close against her waist and divided her figure into two halves. She also wore high-heeled, silver lame shoes. She handed something to Mason, a stack of papers in a file folder. He looked at the material without much interest, and obviously wanted to talk about something else. Kitty laughed and flirted with Mason then abruptly closed the file folder and moved away from him. She walked toward the office and without stopping waved the fingers of her free hand at me. I remained frozen in the act of fitting the brass pieces onto the v-bar of the distribution arm. Kitty opened the office door, went through, and closed the door behind her.

Twenty minutes later she stood beside me clutching her papers. I had been making corrections on the Adam Rice story feeling depressed and confused. The machine had been no comfort to me in this mood, and was acting up, as if to intensify my pain. The distributor had jammed several times, and each time I had climbed to the back of the machine to clear the obstruction, I glanced at the office fearful of what was going on inside. Once, I looked at Mason, and inexplicably, he gave me a thumbs-up sign. I was both amazed and alarmed that Kitty's behaviour was so important to me. We were not in love. My emotional well-being did not depend on what this woman did or did not do. She was not Clare, and she had no power to damage me that way. I was too old, too mature, to wise. I pushed my chair back and looked up at Kitty. I noticed that her face was flushed slightly, and she was frowning.

"What's wrong?" I asked. I stood up, breaking the usual erotic consequences of our position – her breasts opposite my face as I sat, and she stood.

"This place..." she said, and her eyes flickered to embrace the shop. "This goddam Dickens-haunted hole of a place."

"What's that?"

126

I nodded at the folder in her hands. I was curious now, and my anger and hurt subsided a little.

"It's all right," she said. "I'll tell you later."

She turned and walked away, moving straight to the exit door, not pausing, not waving to Mason. As she walked, her body was rigid and straight, unlike I had ever seen her move before.

CHAPTER TWENTY-SIX

"I should have known better," Kitty said.

I had picked up Chinese food, and we ate glumly on the kitchen table, beside the computer. I was prepared for a difficult evening, possibly even a confrontation. I was ready, I thought, to give her back to Mason. In coming to Galaxy Press, Kitty had made an error that astonished me. She had come to get a price on having her office guidebook printed. I had believed that her contempt for Galaxy Press was based on an intelligent understanding of the technology we worked within. Kitty had brought computer printouts of her book, but she had also brought a floppy disk containing the entire book. She expected that the disk could somehow be linked to our letter press equipment and printed on our presses. Only one press could have been used – Sam Storry's offset press. But even that was too limited to do a good book-printing job. And there was no way of using the computer disk. Galaxy Press did not own a computer.

"What did Mr. Goldberg say?" I asked gently.

I was pleased by Kitty's disappointment but could not show it. Her computer literacy was so advanced she had failed to understand a reality that had driven society for half a millennium. I felt superior for a change, and vengeful.

Kitty shook her head. "He said the only way it could be done was on your goddam machine. Then printed on the goddam antique presses."

"You don't want that?" I said.

"No, I don't," she said flatly. "Anyway, it would cost too much and take too long."

I bit into a chicken ball, glad there was some form of justice still alive in the world.

"You could have asked me," I said. "Why didn't you say you were coming in?"

She looked at me. "You would like that wouldn't you?" Telling me how real technology won't work in that stinking dungeon."

I felt a little sick. My jubilation was uncomfortably mixed with jealousy, pain, and fear. And a fading desire to make love.

"I would have enjoyed typesetting your book actually."

"You're serious, aren't you?"

I shrugged. "It's what I do for a living. It's my trade."

We ate in silence for some minutes. The food gathered itself into a lump in my stomach, a submerged boulder the size of Harvey's rock.

"Try Metric Press," I said, finally. "I know they keep up with things."

"Why do you stay there?" she asked. "Just tell me exactly why you stay there."

It was a conversation we had had many times.

"I've got a better question," I said. "Why do you keep going there? What do you want from us?"

Kitty threw down a half-finished egg roll. "I don't want to rush you," she said, "but I'm going out to see the dogs. Liana says Arturo's acting funny."

I almost called Clare that night. In my apartment I had both the television and the radio on, and I sat in my recliner, comfortably surrounded by sound and patters of light. She had a year-and-a-half to see what it was like to live without me. To learn what her new love was like. To discover that her new man belched, farted, had athlete's foot, and left the toilet seat up. To find out that he left mustache clippings in the sink, rolled his socks into balls, and had smelly armpits. She had time to see the passion they must have shared decline to mechanical sex. Premature ejaculation. Erections that died inside her. The abrupt passion of a man emerging from his dreams with a swollen organ, embracing her as if she were a stranger, a whore, a convenient body. All the things she said she hated. Since meeting Kitty, I had not called Clare's number.

Now I pushed the buttons again, prefixing it with the privacy code. And as I had done in the past, I let it ring twice, then hung up. She might guess it was me, or at least wonder. Her always edgy nervous system might provoke an extrasystole in her heart. Or a stab of despair and anger might hit her in the stomach. Or nothing.

The truck stops at an intersection outside the city. It has been a bumpy ride from the open-air market in town, where he slipped into the back of the truck unnoticed and buried himself under an assortment of baskets and corn husks. It was very dusty and dry in this hiding place, but since he does not need to breathe, the conditions do not bother him. Now he slips from the truck and drops to the asphalt road. The truck roars away, leaving him in a cloud of blue smoke. His clothes are covered in dust and silky corn fibers which he does not bother to brush off. To his left is a large, tow-and-a-half story stone farmhouse. Behind it, an old barn blackens in the sunlight. To his right, farther along the road, is a narrow brick church, and behind the church is a cemetery. But he is not draw in that direction. Instead, he steps off the road altogether, and moves toward the sagging wire fence bordering a field of maturing oats.

He must first cross a deep ditch, which is more difficult than he expects, and he falls forward onto the farther bank, breaking his fall with his hands. He struggles over the fence, catching his trousers on the rusty wire. Once, he catches a finger on the wire, where it intersects with a joining link. A small piece of skin is torn from his hand, between the forefinger and thumb, but he feels no pain. Then he is walking through the oats, toward a line of maple trees on the other side of the field. He could lie down in the field, near the trees, and eventually insects and small animals would take care of the rest.

This would be all right, but not if he was aware of what was happening. The idea of a fox carrying away his still conscious head in its mouth does not appeal to him. This idea confuses him, and other images enter his thoughts. He thinks of how it would be to lie beneath the trees, with a woman, kissing her breasts as the leaves whispered above him.

I considered suing Wynford Evans for using my breast-kissing image in his book, but quickly shrugged off the idea. Through the years I had improved many customers' work, and rarely got any thanks for my efforts. It was part of the job which I always thought should have been called a profession. A single fantasy had sustained me over two decades: I would, one day, start a Society of Linotype Operators, with the attractive acronym, SOLO. Membership would be carefully regulated, and SOLO's main function would be to recognize the contribution typesetters had made to literature and language during the machine's hundred-year existence. The society, however, lacked the immediacy of Harvey Wells' new stature as a Drowned Man. Surprisingly, it was Felix Mason who produced the documentation that provided recognition for Harvey. Yet when he drew the poster on a large piece of Bristol board stock, he no doubt meant to ridicule Harvey. The illustration on the poster was ludicrous. In a few quick lines with a black marker, Mason depicted Harvey emerging from a pool of water, holding aloft a dead rat by the tail. Mason had a slight artistic talent – the hastily-drawn figure was unmistakeably Harvey Wells, and the swift, black lines, though simple, were bold and confident, like Mason himself. Below the figure were the words, *Harvey Wells, rescuer of drowned creatures: rats, carboard boxes, and himself.* The contempt was obvious and vicious and to make certain everyone saw it, Mason stapled it over the sink, next to the dirty, framed mirror. Harvey loved it and was so proud of it he scribbled a message on the bottom of the sheet: "Do not discard. Save for H.J.W." It might have been a ruse to turn Mason's contempt back on himself, but I didn't think so. Harvey's admiration for the poster was genuine.

"I like it," he said loudly to Mason. "I really like it – thank you!"

Mason, standing at the Heidelberg platen, stared at Harvey in wonderment. For once, I thought, someone had put Felix Mason off balance, and I felt a strong, savage satisfaction.

When Kitty came into the shop after lunch, she paused to speak to Mason. I watched her from Harvey's stone. The sink was behind the Heidelberg, and the poster caught her attention. She studied it with her hands clasped behind her back. When she turned around, she was smiling broadly. Harvey, happy she had seen the poster, waved at her, and she smiled as she approached the stone. She stopped in front of me.

"Can we go over to your machine?" she said. I nodded and she followed me to my work area where we stood in front of the Linotype, partially concealed from the rest of the shop.

"I took your advice," she said. "I went to Metric Press."

"What did they say?"

"As you said, they can do my book. And they can use my disk, with no problem."

I was relieved. Kitty seemed pleased and happy.

"And they have hundreds of typefaces," she said. "Hundreds more than this place."

I shrugged, expecting this. She reached out and touched my arm.

"Why don't you come over tonight?" she said.

She looked sincere. Her eyes held mine steadily and her fingers were warm on my arm. "They overwhelmed me a bit with their equipment," Kitty said. "I need a little bit of down-to-ear led-pot philosophy." She was mocking me but not without kindness. I felt a surge of weakness and pleasure.

"Are you sure?" I asked.

"Of course. Why wouldn't I be? Come about eight o'clock."

I nodded, and she leaned forward and kissed me on the lips. "See you then," she said and turned and walked away, almost colliding with Mr. Goldberg who was coming out of the office.

CHAPTER TWENTY-SEVEN

Kitty had been determined to enlighten me about computers from the beginning. She had regarded me with an almost missionary zeal that dwindled over the weeks but never completely disappeared. Her error about her book was the lowest point in her campaign, but once she was able to project her embarrassment and frustration onto Galaxy Press, she was able to recover some of her enthusiasm for converting me. We had little else to discuss at an intellectual level. We talked about films and music, agreeing as much as we disagreed, and decision on where to eat became as controversial for us as it was for most couples. But since we did not really see ourselves as a couple, it was easy enough to back away from serious differences of opinion. If we could not agree, we would stop at two restaurants for individual take-out meals. When this happened, we ended up sharing, and the result was often both interesting and amusing. One restaurant we both agreed on was a clean and spacious Greek restaurant called Spano's. we frequently ate there and enjoyed the open atmosphere. But just as often, we brought the meal home with us. We did this shortly after the unpleasant episode of Kitty's error was safely behind us. After we had eaten, and drunk most of a bottle of wine, we relaxed at the kitchen table. Kitty organized the left-over food into the Styrofoam containers, and dumped the scraps into the garbage. I refilled our glasses with wine. Beside us the computer was blank, like a third guest that had gone to sleep. Kitty had wanted to leave it on, but I was determined not to sit in its irritating electronic presence.

"Would you want to eat beside my Linotype?" I said.

She looked as if she were going to argue, then shrugged. A few minutes later she picked up the topic again. "It's simple grammar," she said, switching on the computer. "Your machine is past; my machine is future."

"What happened to the present?" I said glumly.

"The present," Kitty said, watching the screen come to life. "The present is in between. Like purgatory."

"Like what I'm in right now."

She laughed. "Purgatory is where you wait. A place you wait to get out of – eventually."

"How long do I have to wait?"

Kitty leaned back in her chair. "A lot of people have to pray for you," she said. "So make sure you have lot of friends."

"There's you."

"Not me. I'm an apostate."

"So, I'm lost."

"We're both lost. But you more than me."

Kitty stood up and placed her arms on my shoulders. Her cologne was a distant, cool fragrance, a fountain in a courtyard. She moved away, and I stood up.

"See what you've done?"

She pressed her hand against me. "You'll never get out of purgatory that way."

The past and future. Kitty had given me the shape I lived in, a landscape as empty as my daily life. Everything existed in this place: the care and the road I drove it on; the evening ahead; the week that would follow the weekend, and the weeks after that; the inevitable end of Galaxy Press, and Mr. Goldberg's death. All of this was in the foreseeable present, which extended backward into the past and forward into the future. Yet the evening ahead was too pleasant to allow me to become reflective. And the future might not be as bad as I thought it would be. I knew the typewriter keyboard, as well as the Linotype's larger and more spacious keyboard layout. I could operate a word-processor. I could continue to set type if someone would hire me to do it. And if I still needed the lead in y system, I could keep enough Linotype slugs to supply me with what I needed. I could rub the lead on my skin every day or place filings under my tongue. I would certainly carry Linotype fragments with me when I left purgatory. And with a shock, I realized there could only be one direction to go – forward, into Kitty's future. When I told Kitty about the holes the city was digging around the shop, she surprised me with her unexpected interest.

"What are they for?" she asked.

I shook my head. "I'm not really sure. To test the soil composition, I think. Or maybe to look for pressure points."

The city workers had dug one hole right outside the window behind my machine. I leaped out of my chair when the pneumatic drill started on the concrete sidewalk. As usual, my first, momentary reaction was that something had broken on the machine, and I slammed the clutch handle in with the heel of my left hand. Once through the concrete, the digging operation became less noisy, but it was unnerving to feel vibrations on the bottom of my feet as they bored down into the soil with a huge, rotating auger that hung like a dog's phallus from the back of a truck. At one point Mr. Goldberg came to my window and peered out at the workers. He watched them for some time, then turned away.

"What's going to happen?" I asked him.

He stopped and looked at me. The creases in the skin around his eyes seemed deeper, and there was a vacant, almost dreamy expression on his face. "What do you mean?" he said.

"To the shop," I said. "What's going to happen to the shop?"

"I guess you're worried," Mr. Goldberg said.

It was a brief moment of connection between the boss and myself. Mr. Goldberg rarely spoke at length to anyone other than Arnold Clary, and there was seldom any intimacy in our exchanges. But Mr. Goldberg was now looking at me steadily, and with obvious concern.

"I'm doing my best," he said. "But I guess we all have to think ahead a bit." He looked toward the window, then back at me. "We can't really afford renovations. But I want to keep some of the equipment, for a while, at least." He nodded at my machine. "This is one of the pieces I want to keep, and I may need you to help with it. Try not to worry too much." He smiled at me, and moved away quickly, as if to conceal the emotion that was coming over him. He did not wat to lose Galaxy Press, and he did not want any of us to suffer, but it was obvious his resources were running out as swiftly as his energy was waning. He had seen it happen once, in Poland. Now it was happening again. And again, the forces outside the wall of Drukarnia Galaktyka were irresistible and deadly. And perhaps worse, they were inevitable.

"What's wrong?" Kitty asked.

I smiled. "I was thinking about the end of the world."

She laughed. "My God, cheer up! Nobody says you can't have a little fun first."

I raised my eyebrows. "What kind of theology is that?"

"My own," Kitty said.

Shortly after the millennium turned, Professor James claimed at least a partial victory. From the faculty lounge of Oldham College, he gave a news conference that drew a CBC crew, and two newspaper columnists, a turnout that reflected the professor's rapidly fading celebrity. As a prophet he has lost some of his impact, and according to CBC, had only two graduate students in the previous three years. He still taught two or three standard philosophy courses, specializing in Heidegger, and his single elective course on the "origins of thought: a philosophical approach to the formation of literature". His two major books can still be found on some bookshelves, but not in any great numbers. Few magazines publish articles on him anymore, and if the photograph in the *Star* is an accurate image of the man, he has aged significantly in the past five years. During his news conference he made an unexpected announcement, claiming that the value of the printed word had undergone a sea-change, had been eroded and weakened by its dissolution in the ocean of electronic energy. I read this while standing in the magazine section of a grocery store, and promptly brought he newspaper I was holding.

At home I read the article more carefully, and in as great depth as the piece allowed. I felt a curious elation as I read that the professor mourned, "with obvious pain the demise of a technology that had given the word the prominence and stability it deserved – the alchemical process of hot-metal typesetting, and the archetypal, mechanical kiss of type on paper in the controlled power of a printing press that actually pressed images onto the membrane of paper." There was a tiny inset photograph of a Linotype machine which I ran my fingers over lovingly and with great satisfaction, as if I were a stonemason admiring a cathedral I had helped to build. This was a sensation I could now indulge in, and although we seldom expressed such feelings at the Galaxy, it was always present in the background, was part of the reason we remained at the shop.

I once saw a printed book I had typeset at Galaxy Press eleven or twelve years before. There was an annual street exhibition in Toronto hosted by publisher and other groups. An entire street for three or four blocks was closed off and filled with tents and displays and thousands of pedestrians. I wandered through the crowds, but found little of interest, until I stopped to scan a distributing company's titles. I recognized the book instantly. It was a large format, soft-covered book on the history of an outlying area. I picked it up to make sure there was no mistake. It wasn't a reprint, and there were several more copies on the shelf. While typesetting the book I had consulted with the publisher and the writers, trying to solve problems their designs had raised. They wanted the type to go around illustrations and this had required extra work on the Linotype machine. I talked them into reducing the typeface from ten point to nine point, allowing us to use italic figures, which had to be inserted into the machine by hand, since they did not run in the magazines. I must have stood at the booth with the book in my hands for several minutes, remembering particular sections of the text that had given me difficulty, other section that had given me pleasure. I studied the page I had had to reset three times to get the lines to look natural on the right-hand edge, since they wanted the text to be flush on the left but ragged on the right.

"Do you like it?"

I looked at the clerk and nodded. I almost told the young woman about my involvement with the book, but then I would have had to explain, and would probably have ended up sounding like one of the many madmen that roam the streets of large cities – winos, and old printers, like Danny Ellis. Like me. I decided to buy the book, knowing there were no copies at Galaxy Press. I wanted evidence of what I had done, the small part I had contributed to the universe of published books. Craftsmen in all trades leave parts of themselves in their work. Their voices and sweat are in the brickwork of house, the concrete of buildings, the water pipes and electrical wires flowing around us, and they are – or were – in the pages of books, between the line, in the paper, in the words themselves, as much almost, as the authors themselves. I thought of this as I typeset Wynford Evans' opus and was determined to get a copy of the finished book, regardless of its contents. The sound of the jackhammer interrupted my thoughts as yet another hole was started, this time across the street from the shop. I leaned back in my chair and stretched. The telephone in the office rang, activating the bell in the shop. A moment later, Elizabeth Begg came out of the office and marched towards me.

"It's for you," she said disapprovingly, then turned and stalked back to the office.

I felt a stab of anticipation. I no longer received calls at work. Only Clare had done that when we were together. Why would she call me now, after such a long time? Elizabeth was sitting down as I picked up the phone. She breathed heavily through her nostrils, and I knew she was mightily irritated.

"Hello."

"Hi." It was Kitty and I relaxed at once.

"What's up?"

She was silent for a couple of seconds.

"It's Liana," she said finally. "She's dead."

"Dead?" the word when you first hear it, has no meaning, and must be repeated. I heard Kitty's ragged breath in the earpiece and knew she had been crying.

"An accident. It's – awful. I can't talk."

"I'll come over after work," I said. "Are you at home?"

"Took the day off."

"Are you alright?"

You ask questions to kill time and to work around the news. You need to know how to feel, what to feel, and if you are not involved, you must do something for the person who is grieving. And it was obvious Kitty was grieving and had fallen into bottomless despair.

"I took something," she said. "I guess I'll be ok. She was go goddam beautiful."

"I'll come after work."

"Thanks," Kitty said.

"I'll bring something to eat"

"Whatever."

"Alright, Kitty," I said. "I'll see you then."

CHAPTER TWENTY-EIGHT

There were many things we didn't know about each other. Until Liana's accident, I knew little of Kitty's inner dimensions, how deeply she penetrated my psyche, and how emotionally entangled she was with other people who shared her life. Even with Clare, after twenty-three years of marriage, I discovered there were parts of my wife I did not know even existed. I had always thought that what attracted me most strongly to her was what eventually alienated her from me – her strong, quiet sensitivity. An independent, emotional centre that filled her life, but was at the same time sharply isolated from the outside world. I never learned how to live at the edge of that kind of intensity, and finally understood that I never would. I still longed for it, however, and still suffered in its absence. Kitty gave off no such heat. Her intensity was entirely physical, though as powerful as anything I had encountered in a woman. Where this energy came from, I could not imagine. I had no intuitive sense of her character, as I' had with Clare. Unitl the accident.

According to the newspaper report, Liana had been travelling at high speed, and had been dodging in and out of lanes for several miles. It was impossible to know why she miscalculated her final maneuver. Her small care swept under the rear of a tractor trailer, and she, along with her car, was decapitated.

We sat among the paper wrappings and cardboard cartons. Kitty had eaten only half a cheeseburger, and two or three French fries. Her third glass of wine was almost empty. Her eyes were luminous with tears, her skin mottled with sodden make-up. The afternoon newspaper was open on the table to the story of the accident. I was unnerved. I do not handle grief well and something turned liquid inside me as I tried to comfort Kitty. Her pain was stark and frightening. After an hour, when she became quieter, and was sniffling softly, I got up and made some coffee. I kept glancing at her to make sure she was all right. Yet I felt helpless and a little desperate in the proximity of her despair. After an hour of silence, and intermittent tears, Kitty began to talk about her friend.

"The only true friendship I've had in a long time," Kitty said. "We shared our secrets. When the prick she married fooled around on her, she came to me. She even pushed him off onto me, to keep him happy."

I thought of Felix Mason. Did everyone, at some point, give someone away? Had I give Clare away? Had she given me away?

"Were they divorced?"

Kitty nodded and smiled wanly. "Young people don't hack it out anymore."

"Then what?"

"When got married again, and I stood up for her. When she split again I was there to help her."

"Did it work the other way around?

"What do you man?"

"When your affairs broke down, was she there to catch you?"

She smiled warmly. "Of course. But that didn't happen very often."

Night had fallen, and Kitty got up to pull the curtains over the windows. Her movements seemed weaker than usual, and she looked physically beaten and hurt. She sat down again and stared at the blank screen of her computer.

Kitty's pain crippled her for an entire week. She took two days off work, but found the isolation was too much to bear. At home by herself she was restless and inconsolable. The computer, she said, did not offer the solace she thought I would. The timeless intensity she usually experienced on it was no longer accessible. During the two days she went out often, haunting the malls and grocery stores. But she found these places filled with strangers, warm bodies that did not offer warmth, passing psyches that did not acknowledge her existence. Liana's partner on the farm, another young woman, continued to operate the kennels, but informed all the owners that she would soon be selling the property. She told Kitty that there were people interested in buying her dogs. Kitty put the decision off but knew she would probably sell the animals.

"Without Liana there, I don't feel much like going on with it."

She returned to work just to be near the living. My visits in the evenings were a help but I found it difficult to experience her sorrow. Yet perversely, I found her pain reassuring. Somehow, she had acquired more substance, had become less dominating, less authoritative, less in control of our relationship. At first, I held back, wary about moving into the dar, soft space that had opened up in her. But without barriers to stop me, I could not resist her pain, or keep myself from trying to ease her suffering. She accepted my comforting without question and in bed appeared to gain some relief thought physical contact. But as soon as this was past, she fell into an unfamiliar silence, and I could almost sense the other thing taking over her consciousness, the dark thing of pain.

"She taught me a lot," Kitty said, her eyes unfocused on the TV news.

"What did she teach you?" I asked.

"She's the one who taught me about the ethics of oral sex."

"I beg your pardon?"

Kitty smiled, thinking of something in the past, no doubt. "It's not as bad as going all the way," she said pensively. "At least according to Liana. So it's easier to confess."

"But do you think it's actually true?"

"Of course, it's true. Think about it."

I began to visit without phoning first, almost as if I lived there, and as if Kitty was now my responsibility. I had forgotten who we were, who Kitty was. She opened the door tentatively and looked at me wide-eyed.

"It's you."

I nodded. "Yes, it is."

She smiled, then shrugged and opened the door completely. She was wearing a cotton nightgown and her hair was loose. She looked very attractive.

"Were you resting?" I asked.

She shook her head and pointed to the couch. "Do you want a beer?"

Without waiting for an answer se went to the refrigerator and took out two cans of beer. She handed me one and sat beside me on the couch. We might have been married. The casual familiarity was that of a husband and wife. There was not the urgency of lovers, only the acceptance of each other's presence.

"it seems like you're getting back to normal," I said, touching her knee with mine.

Kitty nodded. "Almost."

I heard a sound from the area of the washroom.

"Have you got company?"

She smiled and sipped from the can. "Sort of."

The toilet flushed and the washroom door opened. The sound of slippered feet came toward the living room. Felix Mason emerged from the hallway. He was wearing one of Kitty's robes, an azure flannel gown I had seen Kitty wear occasionally. The sleeves were two inches above his wrists and the front panels of the robe barely overlapped. His chest, with its pale mat of hair, was almost completely exposed.

"Well, well," Mason said. "We have a visitor."

I felt blood filling my face but looked at Kitty and smiled.

"I guess I should have called." I couldn't read Kitty's' expression. She seemed cool, and not particularly concerned.

"It might have been a good idea," she said.

Mason walked flat-footed to the refrigerator and got a beer. He popped the can open and sad down at the kitchen table behind Kitty.

I stood up. "I just came to see how you were," I said. I was determined not to play a role, nor did I know what role to play. A forsaken lover? A betrayed fiancé? An embarrassed suitor? I put the beer down on the glass table beside the touch-lamp. "I'll give you a call tomorrow." Then I looked at Mason. "It looks better on Kitty," I said.

He held his beer can up as if in a toast. He was not in the least uncomfortable. It struck me that we were like characters in a 1040s comedy – two bachelors competing for the same woman finding themselves in a preposterous situation that could only be handled with wry humour and stupid facial expressions. Safely in my care, I found that I was remarkably calm. Mason had had her first, after all. Kitty had been shattered by Liana's death and needed as much comfort as she could get. I provided her with some of it, but apparently, she needed more. Why shouldn't she turn for help where she knew she could get it? We had never made any sort of agreement about our relationship. Why would we expect anything from the other? These were future times and the times demanded flexibility above all things. The century was ending and a lot of conventions had proved themselves to be silly and insupportable, including what men and women did together. From the moment Mason gave Kitty to me she had controlled our relationship. Was Kitty now giving me back after Mason had given her to me? I had no answers, but I felt very tired. That night I called Clare's number and let it continue to ring. When I heard her voice, I hung up.

CHAPTER TWENTY-NINE

"So, you think it was all right for Felix to share you with me?"

Kitty laughed at this, and I felt we had returned to familiar territory.

"Felix," she said, "is incapable of sharing anything with anybody."

The computer was on again during my visits, but Kitty spent less time in front of it. Even when she was fully engaged in a search, or – as she called it – a journey, the duration of her involvement was shorter. I was now unable to finish a complete magazine article if she was on the machine when I arrived, or to watch a full segment of Newsworld. I became aware that she needed my presence, wanted to draw something out of me. It was a new experience, and I was uncertain how to respond.

"Do you want me to move in with you?" I asked. We sat together on the couch, her fingers resting comfortably on my thigh.

"No," she said, without hesitation.

I shrugged. It was as important for me to be detached as it was for her.

"We're at the opposite ends of things," she said. She clung to me, pulled me to her.

"How is work?" I asked, into her hair.

"All right. Getting better."

The period of mourning, and the period of comforting was coming to an end. Mason and I quickly worked out an arrangement, like friends sharing an apartment, inventing a code to warn each other if it was safe to come home or not. Our code, however, was designed merely to avoid our own embarrassment. We both knew Kitty controlled the situation, and more than once she made this clear. She would simply call one or both of us, and explain that she was busy, or had work to do. I knew this meant that Kitty was returning to the computer and had found something in her electronic journeys that made any company unnecessary, or that Mason was planning to visit her.

"I think she's getting back to normal," I said to mason, as I handed him a single Linotype slug to replace the one he had smashed with the press gripper. "What do you think?"

Mason shrugged. "She seems all right." He did not really care and in that respect was as indifferent as Kitty again appeared to be. As Mason lifted the form and slipped it off the stone, the familiar anger and hurt stabbed me briefly. I could not be like them and did not want to be like them. Yet I envied them their hardness. Kitty had been crushed, but the experience did not appear to have changed her in any permanent way. If she had become more vulnerable, or more human, she was managing to conceal the change from me.

"Anytime you want to go and see the dogs, I'll go along," I said to her. The final installment of a ministries based on a Danielle Steel novel had just come to its expected conclusion.

Kitty laughed, and wiped tears from her eyes. "It's not even fucking sad," she said.

"If they had been dogs, I could understand you crying."

She looked at me. "The dogs," she said. "No, I sold the."

"Sorry."

Kitty shrugged. "They hardly knew me anymore." Kitty stood up, and leaned in the direction of the kitchen table.

"You've got work to do," I said.

She nodded and smiled. "A little." I still fantasized, though less frequently, that something would happen to bring Clare and I back together. With Kitty, there was not such hope, or even the need for hope. Our approaching separation was inevitable. I could not think of our friendship with any words possessing qualities of intimacy. We were not in love with each other. Our acts of lovemaking, however, were still lively. Kitty laughed, instructed me, told me erotic stories, and initiated scenarios that always ended in her brass bed.

"Go and put the hat on," she commanded, forcing me to stand up naked from the bed. I went to the hallway and put on her wide-brimmed straw hat. Kitty slammed the bedroom door shut. I stood in front of the door, wear the hat, my manhood foolishly sagging.

"Knock!" she shouted from the bedroom.

I knocked.

"Who is it?"

"Don Diego."

"Come in, Seenyor Diego."

As I stepped into the dark room, she stuck a stiff finger into my back.

"Give it to me," she whispered harshly into my ear.

"Give you what?"

At this point Kitty burst out laughing and pushed me toward the bed. She was laughing so hard there were tears in her eyes. But as we made love, she wiped the moisture away with the same impatient gesture as when she had cried for Danielle Steele. I almost didn't notice that she had been wearing the azure robe that didn't fit Felix Mason.

Without warning Kitty invited Mason and me for dinner. Kitty rarely cooked although she didn't hesitate to put together something fast, fish or chicken, a few frozen vegetables boiled in a pan, a tomato cut up and mixed with dressing. She admitted that a decade of living with a man, she had spent a lot of energy and creativity in preparing meals in great variety and detail.

"That was my green period," she had said. "Never to be repeated."

"Why green?" I asked.

"No reason" she said. "Now it's blue."

She called us separately and told us to bring our own drinks. At lunch Mason and I quickly verified the arrangement.

"Any idea what she's up to?" I said.

Harvey and Sam Storry were with us, but we had gone beyond any concern about appearance, decorum, or worry about their quizzical looks and raised eyebrows.

Mason shook his head. "I guess she wants to lighten things up a bit."

I doubted that and I felt uneasy about the evening ahead. The façade we had established was fragile enough; now Kitty was forcing us to stand side by side, in front of her. I wasn't sure that it could be done. When we got back to the shop, there was a paper taped to the glass panel of the front door of Galaxy Press. We huddled at the door, reading silently.

The city engineer's department has determined that this property and three adjoining properties may be affected by underlying land faults or irregularities. Studies are continuing, and it has been determined that there is no immediate danger to visitors or employees at this address. However, anyone entering these premises should be aware of the possibility of significant problems arising at any time in the near future.

Kitty must have taken the day off to prepare the succession of dishes, starting with a consommé soup, then moving through salad, entrée, dessert, and aperitif. She moved the computer off the table, placing it on top of the counter next to the microwave oven, where it sat like a sibling to the glass-fronted appliance. After setting each dish on the table, she sat down and ate it with us. The only conversation was trivial, and we made many toasts, some of which had to be explained to Kitty.

"Why Ben Franklin?" she asked. "Why Johann Gutenberg?" "Why Ottmar Mergenthaler?" "Why so many Germans?"

This launched mason and I into explanations of the importance of these men in the history and craft of printing. And instead of attacking such reverence, as Kitty usually would have done, she merely giggled and raised her glass to the revered figures, as their names were proposed. We all drank both beer and wine at the same time. Mason also kept a glass of Scotch beside him, and kept up a continuous, and complicated ritual of drinking from all three. By the time Kitty presented her main course, we were well established on the first level of drunkenness, and I knew there could be no turning back. Kitty had cooked a ham, served with a hot, sweet raisin sauce.

"Can't eat ham," Mason said pompously.

Kitty and I regarded him with pretended shock.

"You're no Jew," I said.

"No," Mason said. "But In honour of Mr. Goldberg, I will not eat ham."

"I have a better idea," I said. "Let's toast him."

Mason eagerly accepted that idea and lifted his whiskey glass.

"To the last hero of the century," I said, seriously.

"Saviour of time and tradition," Mason responded solemnly. Mason was not yet completely drunk, and he was more serious than he pretended to be. This was a pleasant change, and I clinked my wine glass against his whiskey glass enthusiastically.

Kitty did not mock us and drank the toast quietly. But we could not sustain the moment. I immediately proposed a toast to Harvey Wells, in what I intended to be an appropriately inflated tone of voice.

"The swimmer who couldn't swim," I said.

"Lover of rats," Mason said. And with his response, Mason turned flat again. The man who minutes ago had honoured Mr. Goldberg, speaking from a depth I had not seen before, had returned to his own surface, which closed over his compassion as if it had never existed.

The supper ended, but we continued drinking. Soon it became clear that this would be an evening dedicated to achieving unconsciousness, an oblivion Kitty denied but obviously needed. In preparing the mean, she had done something for herself, not for us. Our presence served a different purpose, one neither Mason nor I were aware of, but were happy enough to go along with. I had thought it might go differently, but soon saw that Kitty's needs came first. She wanted company, people she could trust to help her escape from her personal, invented purgatory. Later, with the table still covered in dessert dishes and glasses, Kitty mocked the relationship we all had shared, forcing Mason and I to wear her straw hat, and link ourselves together in various combinations to the touch lamp. The game was superficial, however, and we stayed in a state of drunken innocence that would protect us in the morning. I awoke once, or dreamed that I awoke, with Kitty's arms around my neck, breathing heavily in my face. In another dream I saw tow shadows on the floor beside me, wrestling in the darkness.

CHAPTER THIRTY

Strange that he has not considered what is so obvious. Water. The home place of life, and probably its birth. There is only one body of water big enough to satisfy his requirements. The cold lake beside the city. Cold and deep. People often swim across the lake to prove something, to prove that they are strong and alive, that they can recreate themselves by entering it and emerging from it, satisfying perhaps, a need to pass through the birth cycle again. Would the same individuals one day see the lake as he now sees it – as a return to the birthplace, no for renewal, but for dissolution?

It is difficult for him to hold these thoughts for very long in the decaying substance of his brain. In life he had not thought much about such concepts. In life he had acted on impulse, and struggled to maintain his place, or what he considered to be his place. In life he had been merely swimming on the surface, like Marilyn Bell. But unlike Marilyn Bell, he does not want to reach the shore, the blaze of lights. For him, now, there is no shore, there are no lights. This is good. This provides him with the first true sensation he can remember form the past few days. There remains the difficulty of reaching the lake. It lies at the other extreme of the city. At least two changes of bus routes, a trolley line, then another bus route. Although he has picked up coins from the ground whenever he sees them, he has only thirty-three cents in his pocket. He must increase his vigilance, find more money, or another bus ticket. But it is becoming difficult to see clearly. His vision is somehow clotted, or matted, and a shifting film on his eyes makes it difficult to see small objects. Worse, the last time he picked up what he thought was a paper bill, a pigeon bit his hand. He had not seen the bird pulling at what he soon saw was merely a soiled hamburger wrapper. When he looked at his hand closely, he saw that the bird had bitten out a wedge-shaped piece of his flesh. He was perplexed. Why had the bird bitten him, instead of flying off at the approach of a human? Would he now become a target for the hungry creatures that daily forage the air and the earth for scraps of nourishment? Would seagulls dive down on him greedily? Blackbirds? Sparrows? Would mice, cats, and dogs decide to taste his heels and withered flanks?

[ADAM RICE RETURNS TO THE SEA]

The lake, the water, the sea, he senses, is within him. According to something he had heard long before, the blood is very similar to sea water, but he does not know if this applies to clotted, knotted blood, blood that no longer flows, as if the sea and the rivers leading to it were congealed into a single, still essence. Even if the blood did not congeal, it must become still. An interior mirror of the sea. The Alice book had it right about mirrors, the only way to pass into the larger world of the universe. He may once have known this, the literature, the language of the senses. In fact, he does not doubt this. Almost everything is now gone, however, everything except the dark lake of the sea that is now the world his mirror reveals. He has walked in the sun too long. His feet slap on the cement sidewalks, yet there is no evidence that this happens, except that what he sees ahead of him shakes slightly at each step as his body absorbs the shock of walking. More often he looks downwards to see the feet actually make contact with the cement. And this reveals the passing of years to him. The dates are clearly pressed into the cement, usually within the simple shape of a company insignia. There were years in which time was arrested with the life contained in them: 1966, 1970, 1988, yet the life that is there, in the cement, is now remote, does not exist for him. Everything is impression, the possibility of impression. And the sea, somewhere ahead. Any body of water is the sea, as his body is the sea. The old language still comes to his lips, trembles there, like saliva. Water seeks its own level. The world has turned under his feet, moving away from the sun, now low in the sky, approaching the buildings ahead. But the water is beyond. A cry against his ear, from above him. The white, perfect seagull that eats what is dead, and what is going to be dead.

Now he has reached the end of the neatly kept streets with their dark brick houses and dark hedges, their dark windows, and tiny, lifeless lawns. He is confronted by a wide road that in the late afternoon is filling with swift, glinting cars. And with trucks that are larger than trains, and continuous sound that reaches his ears as the rush of moving air. He finds a narrow passageway under the road, a stone tunnel that plunges him into shadow. As he walks the traffic noise falls to a murmur, as mumbled voice above him. The blurred arch of light ahead draws him on, until he emerges again into light and noise. But this time there is a different sound. A hiss. A tongue fluttering on lips. A soft, insistent voice.

The beach is very short, the sand is coarse, the grains becoming pebbles, the pebbles rounded stones. The water speaks in its multi-foamed throat, reclines before him, lying flat, stretching fully to the sky, the liquid line dividing two colours of blue, deep slate and a blue verging into purple. Behind him the traffic's hoarse whisper subsides to something outside his hearing. He knows, abruptly, that his senses have moved from the darkness of his body to the skin, to the pores of his skin, which are now pinpricks in a drawn shade through which light streams, a universe of stars in a rectangular sky. The water soaks his shoes, searching for his skin with its flooding touch. His shoes are off and the water streams over his blackened feet. He now sees the slight curvature of the horizon of water, a vast belly he enters, water splashing into his eyes and face, and pouring down his neck, as if tears were bursting from the openings in his head.

CHAPTER THIRTY-ONE

The feeling that we were at the end of things was everywhere and extended beyond the walls of Galaxy Press. *Fin de siècle* stories had become tiring, however, and there had been so much published and broadcast about the future that we felt we were already in it. In spite of this, there was growing sense of doom around us. Galaxy Press was clearly finished. Mr. Goldberg had begun to miss days at the shop and looked more tired and sickly than ever. He moved through the shop slowly, his skin yellow and dangerous looking. He lingered as he passed among us, pausing to talk briefly, and as he talked, his fingers absently touched his surroundings. At the Heidelberg platen he stroked the embossed letters on the safety guard, as if reading Braille. At the cutting machine, he leaned close to Arnold Cleary, nodding, talking slowly, grasping Arnold's elbow as if to support himself. In the same way he leaned against Harvey's stone, as Harvey prattled brightly about something strange, or insignificant. And when he came to my machine, I pushed in the clutch and sat back in my chair as Mr. Goldberg talked about his love for the Linotype. The first elevator seemed to be his favorite part, and as he stood beside me he covered the top of the elevator with a thin, weak-looking hand. I noticed that his hand was trembling until it found the security of something to hold onto.

Sam Storry had three weeks left before his departure from Galaxy Press, and he had begun to avoid the rest of us. His taciturnity and oddness deepened, and he came out to lunch with us only once or twice a week. Felix Mason must have decided not to allow what he perceived as Sam's impertinence to pass unchallenged. Sam buried himself deeply in the newspaper as he ate, and Mason looked at the page facing him across the table with silent animosity. I could see what was coming. Mason reached

152

out his hand and rapped the paper sharply. Sam jerked in his chair, startled. He laid the paper down and stared at Mason with his mouth half-open.

"Why'd you do that?' he demanded.

"I don't like string at the back of a goddam newspaper," Mason said.

Sam struggled with the situation. His face had become red, and his body twitched. But he was afraid of Mason, afraid to challenge him physically. I thought he was going to get up and walk out of the pub, but he didn't. he still had half a sandwich left and more than half a glass of beer. He was reluctant to abandon his lunch, and instead looked sheepish and angry and worried at the same time.

"Are you going to miss us?" Mason pressed.

"Miss what?" Sam said sharply. "Miss the Jew? Miss that shithole? Miss this loony bugger?" He pointed at Harvey who had his head cocked to one side.

"Do you know who owns the shop you're going to?" I asked him.

Sam glared at me. "What are you talking about?"

"A Jew," I said. "Larry Shapiro, the owner, is a Jew."

Sam shrugged his shoulders and picked up his sandwich. At the same time he tried to glance at the newspaper.

Without looking up, he said, "He's not a pure Jew."

Mason winked at me, knowingly, as if we shared an understanding that Sam Storry could never achieve, nor want to achieve. Sam's stupidity was so colossal we decided to ignore it. He would soon be gone in any case.

In truth Mason and I shared nothing more than the knowledge that we were both Kitty's lovers. And even that was now in doubt. Since the night of the party, the three of us had not met again at the same time. I made certain I called Kitty before I went to see her. We did not talk about that night, and I did not ask Kitty if she was still seeing Mason. And I did not talk to Mason about Kitty. Kitty seemed to have recovered herself fully. Whenever I visited her, the computer was on, and stayed on, and she returned to abusing Galaxy Press, though with the certainty that its days were rapidly running out.

"The world will be a lot safer without all that lead," she said, as we lay flat on her bed, the window, open to the August evening. She turned her face toward me in the darkness.

"What will you do?"

"I'm looking," I said. "And I might take a course."

"In what?"

"Computers," I said. "What else?"

Harvey Wells had entered a dimension of existence the rest of us could only guess at. He had begun to draw upon his entire past life in the creation of his new self. Childhood incidents coloured his stories and appeared to give him new energy. To those around him, it made him seem more than slightly mad.

"See this?" he said to me as I stood at his stone. He held the type from a job he had just unlocked from a form. The type rested on the surface of the stone, and Harvey kept it together with the practiced pressure of his fingers. It was mostly handset type, with a couple of my Linotype slugs at the top. Abruptly, he scattered the type with his hand.

"What's your point?" I said.

Normally, he would have carefully tied the job with string and placed it aside for later distribution into type cases and spacing racks. Now it lay in a mess on his stone. What compositors call "pi".

"Look at it," Harvey said, hands on his hips. "It's a pile of chaos. But out of it can come all kinds of words and shapes and meanings."

I did not intend to follow yet another irregular observation on reality that Harvey now made almost daily, so I said nothing.

"No ideas?" he prodded.

"Who's going to clean it up?"

"Me, of course. In that mess, I'll find a treasure. Maybe some secret meaning."

I once had an uncle who practiced a similar form of madness when he had been drinking. He would stop his young nephews and ask them unanswerable questions, such, as "Why is square functional, and round celestial?"

When we didn't answer, my uncle would try to explain. And when we could no longer hide our perplexity, he would throw up his hand in disgust. "You don't get it, you don't understand, you'll never understand."

Harvey Wells was not like my uncle in any respect except for an inexplicable love of fantasy, and of the operations of his own mind. I don't remember what physical accident had robbed my uncle of his sanity. Harvey, of course, had a reason for his unreason. He had drowned, then had resurrected himself. It was not a surprise when Harvey announced that he was having an end-of-everything party.

"It will be a last supper," he said to mason and me, as the Heidelberg's gripper arm flashed in the air behind us. "A sort of last statement."

"Why?" Mason asked. "Are you going to drown yourself again?"

"We will have hamburgers, hot dogs, whatever," Harvey went on. "Roast dog if you want. I've got a big barbecue."

"And a slimy quarry," Mason said.

Harvey spread the news of his idea throughout the shop. He went into the office and told Mr. Goldberg and Elizabeth Begg. At the cutting machine I heard him tell Arnold Cleary about his plan in a loud voice, and I also heard Arnold say something about sacrilege and blasphemy. But Harvey didn't stop there. Like all of us, he had access to the mechanisms of printing. Each of us, with the help of our fellow printers, had more power than Johann Gutenberg had possessed 500 years earlier. It was the same power anyone with a half decent computer possessed to an even greater degree. Harvey typeset his own invitation by hand, using a 14-point script, a font designed for business announcements, and wedding invitations. When he had completed hand-setting the type, he secured it on a steel galley and pulled good proofs for everyone in the shop. He trimmed the proofs with a razor knife, then handed them out individually. Like a priest, or a mad street zealot, he said the same thing to each person as he gave out the invitations.

"The end is coming."

Felix Mason refused to take the invitation in his hand, so Harvey stood it up on Mason's worktable, behind the Heidelberg. I propped my own invitation on my copy board and read it with resignation.

You are most cordially invited to the Last Proof of Galaxy Press
to commemorate and to celebrate the perpetuation of our ancient
and venerable craft of printing as it is practiced at Galaxy Press
The event will take place at the home of
Harvey James Wells
On Friday, August 20, 1999
At 7:00 p.m.
Food will be provided – bring your swimming
trunks and the beverage of your choice

If the shop was about to collapse, there were no signs of it happening soon. Once the basement flood was cleaned up, there were no repeat floods. The old building seemed as solid as ever, though Arnold Cleary, in his conversations with Mr. Goldberg, learned that it would eventually have to be torn down, along with the neighbouring buildings. These included a shoe warehouse, a three-story office complex, and a furniture store with two levels of apartments above it.

"When is all this supposed to happen?" Mason asked, his foot resting on the frame of the flat-bed press.

It was hard to imagine our morning break area, and its worn furnishings disappearing beneath a wrecking ball.

"In the next year or two," Arnold said.

Arnold was relaxed and calm when he delivered this news. At his age, near retirement, why would he worry about something he could do nothing about?

"What will Mr. Goldberg do?" I asked.

Arnold looked at me. "He's tired, he said. "And sick. Isn't it time he had a rest?"

I felt ashamed for asking the question, yet I had seen no eagerness in Mr. Goldberg to leave the business. He still roamed the shop at closing time, touching the tombstone with his fingers whenever he passed it, as if it were a mezuzah.

"Doesn't any of it bother you?" I asked.

Arnold smiled slightly and nodded. "Yes, it does. But in a way it all fits together."

"How?" I couldn't hide the edge in my voice.

Arnold looked at me and said, almost gently, "You should know – everything is melted in time and used again."

I returned to my machine and sat in front of it. There was no work for me. There were some proofs back from Wynford Evans that had to be corrected, but there was no hurry. Even Elizabeth Begg recognized the truth, finally – that *all* my time was miscellaneous, that Galaxy Press itself was miscellaneous, including her small part in it. My machine was, as Mason had said, just a machine. There were parts of the No. 8 model that invited the caress of human hands. The chrome lever for the clutch was smooth and slender, a silver penis, made for the grip of a palm. The top of the second elevator, in the home position, was at a perfect height for resting the left hand on while considering typographic problems. Standing, the slope of the top magazine invites the operator to rest his open hands on its flat, inclined surface. The delivery slide belt turned incessantly, chattering occasionally, as if in speech. I could now see why Danny Ellis talked to his machine. The No. 8 would have to be scrapped. No one would want it. My machine would be hustled out the shipping door, dragged by a winch into a truck, taken to a wrecker, and destroyed with sledgehammers. I doubted that in spite of his assurance, Mr. Goldberg would be able to keep it. I looked up at the top of the machine, where the brass nameplate was screwed to the frame. Without further thought or hesitation, I pulled my screwdriver form its bracket and stood up on the seat of my chair. It took half a minute to unscrew the plate that had been attached d to the machine for over sixty years. I stepped down to the floor and held the nameplate in my hands. It would do me no good in the years ahead, but it would be mind, and as an *objet du temp,* it held within its molecules the imprint of the machine's vibrations over the years. The letters of the word LINOTYPE were bright brass, the background a dull finish of black paint. I slipped the plate into a shelf behind me, for safekeeping. When I straightened, I found myself staring into Danny Ellis' face. He was leaning on the sill of the open window, and he did not look well. His eyes were read and watery, and although he was three feet away from me, I could smell the sick-grape odour of a heavy wine drinker. He grinned knowingly at me, as if we were old friends, as if we had just taken a break from setting type.

"You busy in there?" he asked.

I shook my head. "Not at all. I think we're just about finished here."

"Have you got a buck or two?"

I reached into my pocket and pulled out some coins. A not-so-amusing thought occurred to me as I dumped the coins into Danny's outstretched hands. It might be a loan I was making to Danny, one I may someday have my hand out to recover, with interest. It was a lie, of course. I was younger and stronger than Danny. I did not intend to surrender as easily as he had. I was a professional worker in words, and I believed this was important, that there was still some demand for literacy in the new age. Danny looked at the money in his hands, then shuffled away from the window wordlessly.

As I sat down again, Wynford Evans came out of the office, and walked vigorously toward me. I grasped the clutch handle and looked up at him.

"It's finished," he said, nodding his head.

"The book?' I asked.

He nodded again. But he had no copy or envelope in his hand.

"He goes into the lake and disappears," Evans said.

"Where's the copy?"

"That's it," Evans said. "Just typeset that: 'He walks into the lake and disappears.'"

Evans turned abruptly, and like Danny Ellis, walked away. I had always suspected that he was not entirely sane and hoped that Mr. Goldberg had got some money from the man for the work I had done on the book. I was not happy with Evans' ending. Although Adam Rice's search for a place to bury himself had amused me, I had nonetheless discovered a certain sympathy for the character. Even a dead man should find some meaning in the world, some comfort. I didn't have to change the magazine, since the Optima type was still loaded, and the mold wheel need only to be turned to the correct position. I quickly se the line measurements. I decided to add something to Wynford Evans' last sentence. He had used my words once; he might accept them again.

Adam Rice walks into the lake. Before he disappears, he becomes aware of the water's warmth. The water feels as if a giant has urinated into it.

CHAPTER THIRTY-TWO

Mr. Goldberg sat on a flat rock ledge, fully clothed, his bare feet dangling motionless in the water. Harvey swam vigorously around the edge of the quarry, as if trying to recreate the current he said had pulled him down. His wife sat in the weeds at the highest point of the quarry's edge, a dreamy, simple expression on her face. Felix Mason sat with his date at a wooden table on the lower ground, near the water. He was drinking seriously and running his hand along a woman's thigh. She was much younger than Mason, probably in her early thirties, and quite attractive. She looked intensely bored by the party. Arnold Cleary stood like a skeleton not far from Mason. His bathing trunks were baggy, and even from a distance, his flesh looked ravaged on his bones. To one side of Arnold, Sam Storry and his wife stood in ankle-deep water and splashed each other in an attempt at playing. I had no doubt they would act the same way at a beach, or in their own back yard, or anywhere there was water, and they could find nothing else to do. Sam's wife was a pleasant-looking woman, with short, stocky legs. She didn't seem interested in talking to anyone but her husband. Elizabeth Begg was sitting in the fabric lawn chair she had brought, reading a book, shading her eyes from the sun with one hand. It was almost eight-thirty, and the sun was moving rapidly toward the row of trees half a mile away. We had eaten early, in Harvey's large back yard, and it was good to have that part over with.

Harvey's idea of our last meal together was hamburger meat, and large, doughy buns that tended to fall apart when you tried to bite into them. Harvey wore a glossy vinyl apron on which a giant pig grinned hideously, cooking tongs in one hoof, and a gleaming knife in the other. The pig, which looked almost human, also wore an apron, with red, sizzling letters on it, announcing, "Let's eat!" Harvey happily burnt everything on his hand-made barbecue, but no one complained. Our mood was subdued and heavy. Only Harvey was happy, and it was difficult to know if he was acting, merely nervous, or genuinely, insanely, cheerful. Alice hovered around her husband, handing him meat and buns whenever they were needed. Other than greeting us briefly with a tired smile, she said little, and was as morose as everyone else. While they were eating, Mr. Goldberg and Elizabeth Begg sat on one side of the rough wooden table, Arnold Cleary and is wife on the other. The rest of us sat on the ground on blankets Alice Wells had spread out for us. Kitty an I sat beside Felix Mason and his date. As soon as the chore of eating was finished, Harvey urged us toward the quarry. He asked Felix and me to help him carry two large halogen lamps to the high edge of the quarry, while he unwound the extension cord from a portable, wheeled device.

"We have to do this in style," he said, as he paid out the yellow cord like a fisherman on the end of a net.

We placed the lights bout 25 feet apart, and Harvey positioned them so that they pointed down at the water and the flat, sloping approach to the water's edge. It was still early, and he could not test the effect of the lights yet, but he appeared to be happy with their arrangement. A group of teenagers were swimming in the quarry as we set up the lights, and when they saw the straggling group of adults arriving, they looked at us sullenly and defiantly. Harvey waved to them cheerfully, and this was too much for them. They left ten minutes later. I had not expected to stay until darkness, but Kitty was in no hurry to leave. I grew increasingly uneasy as she talked and joked with Mason and his date. Mason had introduced her as Ellen, and she reminded me of an older version of Liana, a resemblance that brought on a prickly sensation in my scalp. Ellen was vaguely irritated by Mason's obvious closeness to Kitty, but her annoyance was lost in a greater indifference and boredom that probably included more than the weary entertainment at the quarry.

Kitty, on the other hand, was fascinated by it all.

"Look at your boss," she said, nodding her head in the direction of Mr. Goldberg, who kicked his feet listlessly in the water.

"He looked like he'd like to drown himself," she said

"Why do you say that?" I said. "He's not a well man, you know."

Kitty looked at me and shrugged. Tiny creases at the corners of her eyes revealed the humorous mood she had been in since we arrived.

"Do you want the truth?"

"I hate people who insist on telling the truth," I said.

Ignoring my comment, she went on, "I think the whole lot you should drown yourselves in there."

I made a grab for her, and she shifted away, laughing.

"Want to go in?" I asked.

"Sure," she said. "I'm ready."

She rolled down the top of her slacks to show me her bathing suit.

"Better wait a bit, thought," she said. "You know, two hours after eating."

The sun had touched the trees, and I was grimly determined not to stay much later. Then Harvey's lamps came on. We sat almost directly opposite them, and they flared painfully into our eyes, though they had little effect on the lingering light in the sky above.

Harvey stood between the lights, and danced a little jig, as if proud of his accomplishment.

"As soon as it gets dark," Kitty said, resting a hand on my knee, "we'll go in."

The water was chilly at first, but our bodies quickly adapted, and the night air became cooler on the skin than the water that engulfed us. Kitty and I entered the water at the flat end of the quarry, from the ramp originally used by trucks to haul rock from the jagged, circular hole. Seen from above, the quarry must have resembled a large cup, with one end flattened down, as if designed for a giant infant to drink from. Only Harvey was in the water with us. He was doggedly swimming around the circumference of the quarry, while everyone gathered on the rocky ramp. Much of the time he was lighted by the lamps above the quarry, but at the far edge, he disappeared into the darkness, and I wondered if, like an astronaut on the far side of the moon, he would emerge again. No one wanted to dive down into the quarry's dark depths to rescue him. Alice Wells now stood very close to the edge of the water, obviously nervous and fearful. Once Kitty and I were in the water, Alice relaxed somewhat, and the others began talking in louder voices. Their words came out to us easily over the surface of the water, and I could hear Felix Mason's cynical laugh rise clearly into the night. We swam out to the middle of the quarry, a distance of only thirty or forty feet. There we paused and held each other's arms and tread water. We could hear Harvey puffing and snorting as he circled around us.

"Is this – where he went down?" Kitty said, her voice shortened with exertion.

"Don't know," I said.

Harvey had said the quarry was ten to fifteen feet deep near the middle, and in the night, the thought of that much water beneath us was not comforting. Yet we were curiously buoyant, holding each other and stoking steadily with our legs. We heard a splash, and I saw that Mason and Ellen had plunged into the water and were swimming side by side toward the far end of the quarry.

"Let's go..." Kitty said. "In the shadows."

We moved easily into a side stoke, so that as we swam, we were facing each other. Within seconds, we crossed Harvey's path, and he glared at us, his face strained with exertion, his eyes reflecting the lights, his mouth distorted hideously as he gasped for air. But he managed to grin through his effort as we passed him.

"Great, eh?" he said, his voice garbled by the water. Then he was gone, heading for the ramp. Abruptly we were in the shadows, out of the lights' glare. We stopped, and continued treading water, holding each other. From this position we could see the rest of the quarry, and the party gathered on the ramp, where Harvey now emerged, panting, and shaking himself vigorously. On the other side of the water Mason laughed out loud, his voice sounding very close. Kitty put her hand down the front of my bathing trunks and held me warmly. I had to support her as she struggled in the water.

"Here," she whispered, and I was sure her voice carried across to the other side of the quarry. She kicked toward a shelf of rock at the edge of the quarry, and I followed. She still held me securely in her hand. At the shelf we could rest our elbows while we removed our trunks. I didn't think it was possible, but Kitty had me fully aroused in the water. I tried to resist, fearful of being discovered, but we were quickly beyond that point. We placed our bathing trunks on the ledge and positioned our bodies in the dark water. When I was inside her we pushed away from the rock shelf and floated in the water. It was not possible to move against her without sinking.

"Take a breath," I gasped.

We sank below the surface as we pushed against each other, Kitty's legs wrapped around my buttocks. It was difficult to know if we were sinking deeper. Our concentration and movement became regular and effortless. An underwater wee brushed against my leg. Bubbles broke form Kitty's mouth inches from my ear. Our bodies were warm in the water, and the water itself was warm and black. I did not think I would finish, nor did it seem important. More weeds touched my skin, and my buttocks struck against the rocky bottom. A fine, loose grit covered the bottom of the quarry, and grated against my skin. A glimmer of light moved in the water, and I saw the faint pallor of Kitty's skin, a watery glimpse of her pale breast. The light shifted and stabbed dimly in the water, and I realized Harvey must be looking for us. Without meaning to, I had slipped out of Kitty, and finished in the water. There was very little sensation, a mere tightness in my pelvis. We separated and rose quickly, lungs straining for air. We broke the surface gasping and swam for the rock ledge a few feet to our right. Harvey must have heard us and swung on of the halogen lights in our direction. We kept our bodies in the water as we struggled to get back into our suits. Someone jeered from the shore, and Harvey made a childish taunt from the top of the quarry.

Abruptly, Mason was beside us, blowing water from his mouth. Close beside him Ellen stopped, and tread water.

"Did you find it?" Mason yelled.

"What – find *what?*" I yelled back.

"Harvey's other rock. Weren't you looking for it?" He laughed, a curious, strained chortle, then turned and swam away, Ellen following. The water had become chilly again, as Kitty and I swam to the ramp area. Mr. Goldberg and Elizabeth Begg had already walked to the top of the slope, and others were preparing to leave. Harvey was nowhere in sight and the lights suddenly went out, plunging the quarry into deep darkness. For a moment I felt a loss of equilibrium. The quarry behind us was black, the slope on which we stood only dimly visible. The Kitty grasped my arm, and I got my bearings again. The rough ground hurt my feet as we walked to the dark patch on the ground that was our clothes. I felt like a fish, confused about whether I should be in the water or out of it. The party, thank God, was over.

CHAPTER THIRTY-THREE

Although Mr. Goldberg was running out of money, he decided that we would print Wynford Evans' book. For the first time I was Arnold Clary openly criticize the man he had worked for since the early fifties.

"Why would he waste money on that fool?" Arnold said angrily, during the break.

"Have you read any of The Odyssey of Adam Rice?" I asked him.

Arnold shook his head. "Just the occasional proof. That was enough. Besides, I've read the original *Odyssey*."

"Horseshit," Mason said. As usual, Arnold ignored Mason.

"There must be a reason he wants to print it," I said.

"I guess he wants to do one last book," Arnold said, "have the last word."

Wynford Evans did not appear in the shop again. But we continued to work on his book, which was very slim, and to charge time on the docket number. There wasn't much left for me to do, except the occasional correction, the front pages, and the folio numbers. Harvey had begun to make up my Linotype lines into pages, and because he was so efficient, he quickly reached the end. Twenty pages. In forms of four pages each, there would be only five forms to prepare for the press, plus one four-page form for the front pages.

"Piece of cake," Harvey said off-handedly.

It would be a soft-cover book, trimmed and glued in a perfect bind. For the presswork, Mr. Goldberg wrote the number of copies boldly on the front of the docket: 100. The stock was to be Lockhaven Eggshell, No. 1033. The pressman would be Felix Mason, our resident Heidelberg man.

"I hope your type stands straight this time," Mason said, when he got the docket.

"Fuck off," I said to him. Somehow, I could say this easily to min, without fear or hesitation. And I was able to say it flatly, they way Mason himself spoke. It was a comforting way to speak, without excessive energy, and with no thought for the consequences.

For the cover of the book, Mr. Goldberg had chosen an image from a Diego Rivera mural, depicting a man peering through the eyes of a death's mask. He had to send the drawing to Toronto to have the cut made, insisting that all the printing be done letterpress, from raised surfaces.

"The cut will probably be made by a computer," Sam Storry said contemptuously.

"You don't understand anything," Arnold said to Sam.

Sam shrugged. It did not matter to him. He was leaving at the end of the day.

I still have the last lines that I typeset on the No. 8 Linotype machine just before Galaxy Press closed down four months later, in the first month of the new millennium. There are only 10 lines, set in 12-point Times Roman, which I keep on top of the stereo, tied together with string. The proof I pulled from the type is framed and mounted on the wall above the stereo. By putting the fantasy into words, I hope the reality will follow.

> T.S., a typesetter, has recently reunited with his former wife, Clarice, in a small ceremony shared by friends and colleagues. Present at the event were former co-workers, Felix Mason, Arnold Cleary, Elizabeth Begg, Harvey Wells, and the late Messrs. Simon Goldberg and Adam Rice. Regrets were received by Samuel Storry and Wynford Evans. Matron of Honour for the ceremony was Katherine Travis, who presented the couple with a handsome brass touch-tamp. They will spend the first year of the century attempting to recapture the time they lost.

SYNOPSIS OF *GALAXY'S END*

Galaxy Press is an "old era" printing shop. It continues to use hot metal typesetting and letter press printing in the last year of the twentieth century, while everywhere else computer technology has revolutionized the graphic arts industry.

The company is owned by Simon Goldberg, a survivor of the Holocaust, who finances the shop in an effort to keep alive the memory of his family's printing company in Poland before the Second World War. The original company's name was Drukarnia Galaktyka – Galaxy Press.

The narrator is a Linotype operator. Along with the other printers at Galaxy Press, he practices the trade he knows has been transformed in the world beyond the shop. He is pulled into the present and the future by his relationship with Kitty Travis, a woman who is preoccupied by computer technology and its promise. Kitty provides solace for the Typesetter's loss of his wife Clarice, through divorce.

Kitty – a Hecate figure – is an advocate of the information age. An executive assistant in the workplace, she is contemptuous of Galaxy Press and its efforts to resist progress. Before her friendship with the typesetter, she has had a relationship with one of the pressmen in the shop – Felix Mason.

A pivotal even in the story is the near-drowning of Harvey Wells – another of the printers – in a quarry near his home. This event, and the character himself, focuses the opposing energies of the novel, and provides a central metaphor for the themes of change, loss and sorrow.

The wanderings of a fictional character, Adam Rice, are typeset by the narrator on his Linotype, and counterpoint the broader themes of the novel.

As the year (and the century) ends, Galaxy Press's days are numbered. Mr. Goldberg is in declining health, and his financial resources are dwindling; a land fault endangers the shop itself; and the characters have begun to face the realities of the times. A final meeting, or party – a "last proof" – is held at the home of Harvey Wells.

The resolution of the novel is ambiguous, but not without hope. The characters have begun to accept the reality of their situation, of the necessity for change, and the pain such change will inevitably bring. Yet, in spite of this, they manage to sustain the unchanging essence of their own individuality.

Thematically, *Galaxy's End* attempts to depict the moment civilization slips from the substance of reality (hot-metal printing) to the insubstantial essence of digital technology. The theoretical significance of what is happening is provided by reference to Professor Carter James – a McLuhanesque figure – and his writings on "the sacred word" – a satirical position engaging the ideas of Marshal McLuhan.

GALAXY'S END
THEMATIC COMMENTS

The Typesetter's love of his work, his relationship with his machine, is not unusual. Like many tradespeople, he views the world around him from his machine; he experiences reveries at the machine's keyboard; and on his machine he is in touch with the 500-year-history of his craft. The substance he works with is a metal of the earth – lead – at once solid and heavy, but in its molten state possessing alchemical powers of transformation.

The Typesetter's lover, Kitty, lives within an opposing medium – the electronic realm of the computer technology. They are contemptuous of each other's worlds yet share the physical and psychic domain of sexual passion.

Their relationship represents the polarities of past and future, masculine and feminine, and passivity-assertiveness. The novel searches for a resolution of these differences.

The character Harvey Wells brings energy and depth into the story's setting, and through his behaviour and experience, offers possibilities for understanding, if not resolving, the tensions between the main characters.

AUTHOR'S COMMENTS

"My new novel, Galaxy's End, deals with the effects of change at the end of the Twentieth Century, and fits into the flourishing market of fiction and non-fiction books on this theme. In the final year of the Millennium the characters of Galaxy's End live in denial of the computerization of the printing craft, accomplished decades before.

> *My own experience as a typesetter through the sixties and seventies give me intimate knowledge of the 'old era' hot metal printing trade as it is depicted in the novel. The revolutionary changes in the trade symbolize what has happened, and is happening, throughout the working world."*

— David Andrus, MA (English), B.Ed.

GALAXY'S END CHARACTERS

SIMON GOLDBERG owns Galaxy Press and devotes all his resources to holding the company in the past. As a teenager in Poland, he worked for his family's printing company, Drukarnia Galaktyka. Both the business and most of his family were lost in the Holocaust. Mr. Goldberg and his sister managed to survive and emigrated to Canada. Here Mr. Goldberg attempts to recreate what had been destroyed in Poland.

"THE TYPESETTER" narrates the novel. Galaxy Press provides the security he lacks following the break-up of his marriage. His relationship with Kitty Travis brings the two poles of the novel into sharp confrontation: the desire for a changeless existence, and the reality of daily, ceaseless change.

KITTY TRAVIS is an independent woman, who enjoys the information revolution, and spends much of her time exploring the universe of the computer. Emotionally and sexually independent, her views disturb the Typesetter's not-so-safe corner at Galaxy Press.

HARVEY WELLS is a compositor and a "stone man", who makes up type and locks it into forms for printing on the presses. Harvey is an eccentric, trickster figure who suffers near-death by drowning. His experience brings the dynamics of change into the heart of *Galaxy's End*.

FELIX MASON, a pressman, is a self-sufficient individual, who is focussed on the present, with little concern for the future. A former lover of Kitty, he continues to be active in the narrator's relationship with her.

SAM STORRY is a pressman who is restless and uncomfortable at Galaxy Press and decides to leave and carry on his trade elsewhere, and to keep up with new technology. His racist views on working for a Jewish owner express the ambiguities of an idealized past.

ARNOLD CLEARY is an older man, a printer who does various jobs around the shop, and who is a sympathetic ally of Mr. Goldberg. He represents an important perspective of wisdom and acceptance in the novel.

ELIZABETH BEGG is the firm's secretary. She is a severe, nervous woman, intensely loyal to Mr. Goldberg. Her inflexibility is characteristic of many individuals facing change.

ADAM RICE is a "fictional" character, the creation of WYNFORD EVANS, a customer who brings a manuscript to Galaxy Press for printing. The Adam Rice story is a fantasy about a man who has died, yet continues to dwell in the surface world, seeking an appropriate grave. This sub-story is brief and is interspersed throughout the novel. It is typeset by the narrator on his machine and counterpoints the novel's themes.

DANNY ELLIS is an infrequent character, an older man who is a casualty of the computerization of the printing trade and was unable to adapt to the changes. He is typical of those who have been damaged in today's marketplace.

DAVID ANDRUS
PUBLISHED WORK

Fiction	**THE OCEAN TREE** – Novel	(Oberon Press, 1994)

Fiction **THE OCEAN TREE** – Novel (Oberon Press, 1994)
ISBN 88750 976 3 HC
ISBN 88750 968 1 SC
1995 Hamilton and Region Arts Council Award of Excellence

Short **Periodical Publications**
Fiction *University of Toronto Review*
Journal of Canadian Fiction
The Canadian Author & Bookman (Okanagan Short Fiction Prize)
Wascana Review
Weave & Spin (Mini Mocho Press, 1990)
The Golden Horseshoe Anthology (Mini Mocho Press, 1992)
The Hamilton Spectator

Poetry **IN THE BEGINNING WAS** (Oberon Press, 1989)
THE WORD
ISBN 88750 753
Canadian Literature (Vol. 130, Autumn, 1991) – review

WORM COUNTY (self-published, 1980)
This collection of poems contains work that was published in a
number of literary periodicals including: *The Antigonish Review; The
Canadian Author & Bookman; The Canadian Review; Fiddlehead;
Harvest; Nebula; Poetry Toronto Newsletter; Origins; Rikka; Waves;*
and the Coach House Press Anthology, *This is My Best.*

Awards 1981 – Excellence in the Arts (Poetry), Hamilton Creative Arts
Association, and CJJD Radio.

1987 – Okanagan Short Fiction Award, The Canadian Author &
Bookman.

1995 – Award of Excellence, Hamilton and Region Arts Council
for *The Ocean Tree.*

GALAXY'S END

by David Andrus

DAVID ANDRUS (1940 – 2019)

David Andrus was one of the last typesetters of his trade and his love for the Linotype and the English language permeated every aspect of his life. A published author and poet, David is survived by his wife Delisa, daughter Kimberly, and granddaughter Lisa.

He was born and raised in Hamilton, Ontario where he ended his career as a printer and subsequently attended McMaster University obtaining his Master's in English. After printing David worked at Canada Post in Corporate Communications, was a High School English teacher, and helped in raising his devoted granddaughter Lisa.

This novel was written by David Andrus and published by his daughter who admired her father's intelligence and creativity and who misses him dearly.

"Everything is melted in time, and used again..."

CPSIA information can be obtained
at www.ICGtesting.com
Printed in the USA
LVHW030809181221
706565LV00015B/312

9 780228 860532